Time Like a River

by RANDY PERRIN

with Hannah Perrin & Tova Perrin

RDR BOOKS and
ORCA BOOK PUBLISHERS

Time Like a River is a copublication of RDR Books and Orca Book Publishers.

Canadian Cataloguing in Publication Data
Perrin, Randy, 1952
Time like a river

ISBN 1-57143-067-9

I. Perrin, Hannah, 1986– II. Perrin, Tova, 1984– III. Title.
PS3566.E6955T56 1997 j813'.54 C97–910435–1

Front cover illustration and design by Ken Campbell
Printed and bound in Canada

RDR Books
4456 Piedmont Avenue
Oakland, CA   94611
USA

Orca Book Publishers
PO Box 5626, Station B
Victoria, BC V8R 6S4
Canada

Orca Book Publishers
PO Box 468
Custer, WA 98240-0468
USA

99 98 97   5 4 3 2 1

Dedication

To the Daniels-Levinson family, Sally, Doug, Danielle and Charlotte who brought us to Ardenwood for a May Day celebration in 1993 and were there when the foal, *Time Like a River* was born.

To Suzie McLean-Balderson's third-grade class of '94-95 at Park Day School in Oakland including: Eric Baxter, Emma Bernstein, Milani Butticci, Safiya Carter-Thompson, Elisa Castro, Nigel Daniels, David Ebong, Amy Ensign-Barstow, Bradley Johnson, Rachel Lee, Julian Lloyd, Richard Newman, Alexandra Pauley, Hannah Perrin (one of the authors), Madeline Phillips, and Gabriel Rodriguez. Suzie used the book in her class, reading it to the class over a period of a couple months. The kids offered their criticisms and suggestions and Hannah brought them to the other authors for consideration. We apologize for the parts of that early draft you loved that are no longer there.

Finally, to Karen Tanner who, perhaps unfairly, was the only one in the family who got no credit for writing the book. Karen was the person who helped keep the process a positive one for all of us, ensuring our collaborative process was respectful and supportive.

< 1 >

TREMORS

I have an image of my mom. She's dancing around in a circle, singing something. She's beautiful, tall and smiling. Her reddish-blonde hair bounces as she spins and her voice is sweet, clear and high.

There's sunlight coming through a window behind her and she moves in and out of it, turning and spinning with the music. I see that my mom is holding something, a baby. She's bending forward, singing a song. I still remember how she sang it:

It's only love and that is all.
Why should I feel the way I do?
It's only love and that is all.
And it's so easy loving you....

It wasn't until I was nine or ten years old that I found out the real words were " ... it's so hard loving you."

But everything was easy for Mom. She was perfect. That's how I saw her for most of my life. I must have been perfect back then, too — at least when I was a baby. Of course by the time I was listening to the Beatles, I knew the real words and I knew I wasn't perfect. I wasn't popular, I wasn't as good in school as

1

Mom and Dad thought I should be, and, finishing up my twelfth
year on this planet, I had developed what my father, Neil Belzer,
called "a real attitude."

Then, while I was studying for my Bat Mitzvah, I found
out my mother, who'd never been sick a day in her life, was
suddenly very sick and getting sicker.

～～～ ～～～ ～～～

"Margie?" It was my father, calling from downstairs. I
stopped typing on my computer and turned toward the
open door.

"In my room," I yelled.

While Dad clumped up the stairs, I took another look
at what was the start of my first novel. I could already see
the title wasn't any good. "The Trouble with Time" just
sounded clunky. I needed something a little snappier,
more mysterious.

Dad was already upstairs and standing in the doorway
and I hadn't thought up a new title yet. I had twenty pages
of a school report almost ready to drop in the middle of
the book and a bunch of diary entries to type in. Add to
that the first page I'd just completed and I had — a long
way to go. There was plenty of time for me to figure out a
new title.

Dad was wearing a dark green sweater and blue slacks.
His brown hair was messy with white patches. I had to
look closely before I realized the white was flour. Dad
had been baking.

"The mail came," he said, stepping over to my desk.
"Here's a letter for you from Palo Alto."

I took the envelope. Dad was staring at my computer
screen.

"You're working on your book?" he asked.

I nodded as I examined the envelope.

"I'll bet that's hard. I never much liked writing in
school. I guess that's one of the reasons I got into con-

2

struction. I can build with boards and nails — words are entirely too slippery."

"Actually, it's not at all like I'm writing for school," I said, "The story is just pouring out of me as fast as I can type. Of course, that's not very fast, but it's like the story wants to be told." I smiled. "I do wish I could type faster."

Dad shook his head. "Well, don't worry about your typing. By the time you've written a book you'll be better at typing and at a lot of other things." He smiled. "It's nice to have some talent in the family. You must have gotten it from your mother."

I'd been flipping the envelope over, like I was looking for some hidden clues. Finally I slipped my finger under the flap and tore it open. Dad stood there watching, but as I looked up at him there was a strange look on his face. I guess he felt uncomfortable about the letter, too. I'd asked Dr. Albers some pretty specific questions about what had happened to my mother and at that moment I wasn't sure I was ready for her answers.

"Well, I guess I'd better get downstairs," he said as I slowly unfolded the letter. "I've got some rolls in the oven. I wouldn't want to get distracted and burn them. Wouldn't that be just like me?"

I nodded to him and turned my attention to the letter.

Dear Margie,

First, I want to thank you for your help and to assure you that I am honored to address your questions. We certainly owe you a debt of gratitude for the help you gave us. I want you to know that the Center for the Treatment of Infectious Diseases has access to the latest diagnostic equipment and tests, and that our diagnostic team is second to none. Nonetheless, in many ways we're prisoners of our training and our expectations. Sometimes we rely on tests when we should be relying on our brains and our intuition.

You asked for some medical details for your book and I'm

*going to provide them, though I do so with some reluc-
tance, knowing how much you've suffered already. On
the other hand, I believe writing this book will be good
for you in helping you put events into perspective. Anyway, here are excerpts from your mother's medical chart:*

Presenting Symptoms: *Rapid, progressive, neurological
degeneration, evidenced by increasing loss of fine and
gross motor control, including tremors in the extremities
(her shaking hands).*

MRI Scan: *Diffuse areas of dismyelination and demy-
elination in the deep white and cerebellar white matter
(referring to the progressive nerve damage).*

*I hope this helps you better understand the medical side
of things.*

*You must tell us when your book comes out. All of us at
the Center are consumed with curiosity. That you were
able to point us to the cause of your mom's illness was
incredible enough, but the way you arrived at it …! As a
doctor, I've been trained to think in very concrete terms,
but I know I've spent more than one night staring at the
ceiling, wondering at your fantastic adventure. Your
story, which is certainly a story of profound love and
courage, tests my fundamental assumptions about life
and reality.*

*I wanted to tell you a little about your mom as a patient.
Patients can be awful. It's hard to blame them. They're
sick and they want to be anywhere but a hospital. Sometimes they even blame their doctors for the disease. Not
Shelley Gould though. Your mother was wonderful! Even
during the worst of times, she kept a positive attitude and
a smile …*

I shivered involuntarily and looked away from Dr.
Alber's precise handwriting, unwilling to read anymore. In
my mind I could see Mom's smile on the day Dad dumped

me at school and took her down to Palo Alto, and I could see the "tremors in the extremities," the shaking of her hand. It started me thinking again of the whole nightmare that began the night of my thirteenth birthday.

∿∿ ∿∿ ∿∿

It was a Saturday night and I was with Mom and Dad at Mar-Jee's Fine Mandarin Cuisine, my favorite restaurant. I wasn't having a regular birthday party mostly because I didn't really have that many friends, but all the omens seemed right for the start of my thirteenth year.

I was excited about turning thirteen. I guess change can look pretty good when things around you aren't going so well. Being twelve was like wearing too-tight shoes. I wanted bright, new Reeboks with flashing lights in the heels. I wanted shoes that squeaked or tapped when I walked, that told the world I was there. I wanted to be grown up, to put my childhood behind me — and I didn't want to wait.

Dinner was great — especially the mu-shoo vegetables wrapped in little pancakes. It all tasted better here than when Dad brought it home in the little, white boxes hanging from wire handles. Maybe it was the red curtains at the end of the booths, the plates with the pagodas and roosters or the blended smells from the kitchen. Maybe it was just because it was my birthday that everything seemed so right. Even the little Chinese girl who kept appearing and disappearing in the corners of the restaurant and around the tables added to the excitement of my birthday dinner.

She was cute — dark eyes and short-cropped, shiny black hair. She was wearing a white dress with cranes and twisted trees embroidered around the hem. She must have been five or six years old. Off and on during dinner I saw her, peeking at me, always looking away just as I glanced up.

We had finished eating and were talking about my upcoming Bat Mitzvah. A Bat Mitzvah celebrates the time when a Jewish girl turns thirteen, old enough to participate in the Jewish community's rituals. It can be almost as big a deal as a wedding, with a ceremony, a lunch or dinner, and sometimes a party. It was normally a difficult subject in our house because of the expense and because of the preparation I had to do — which I was putting off. Dad was joking that he'd invited all the boys from Willard Junior High to come hear my speech.

"And what's more, Margie, they're all coming!" he said.

I scowled theatrically. Then we all laughed. That was the moment Mom reached for her teacup. For some reason, Dad and I stopped what we were doing and watched her.

Mom's beautiful, perfect hand, her thin, tanned fingers that were so strong and capable, reached forward and paused, inches short of the cup. Mom stared as if her hand belonged to someone else. A tiny tremor started in her fingertips, just a shiver, but it grew and spread down to her hand and wrist. Mom opened her hand and pushed it flat on the table to stop the tremors, her fingers spread out and tense. Someone must have come in the restaurant just then, because I felt a draft of cool air.

After a couple seconds, she lifted her hand from the table and completed the motion she had started, picking up the teacup and drinking as if nothing had happened, but she saw my expression.

"Now what do you suppose that was all about?" she asked, smiling uncertainly.

We were heading out the door when the little girl who'd been watching me came running up with a fortune cookie.

"Here. Please! You have forgotten your fortune. It is most important." She was so serious, as if I'd left my watch or purse or something valuable. I thanked her and she

. 6

made a tiny, quick bow turning back to the kitchen door where a woman, probably her mother, stood watching us.

"Why did she say I forgot my *fortune?*" I asked. "Why not *fortune cookie?*"

"It must be your 'most important' special birthday fortune," my father joked, giving me a hug.

I expected to find something like "You will have a great birthday" or "You will do well at your Bat Mitzvah" some kind of inside joke. So when I cracked it open I was surprised to find I couldn't read it at all. It had two strange looking characters that looked handwritten — in Chinese.

"Okay," I said handing it to my dad, "What's it say?"

Dad took it from me and turned it over a couple times, looking at it closely.

"Can you beat that? I've never seen a fortune written in Chinese before. Maybe the little girl wrote it. She sure seemed to be taken with you."

‹ 2 ›

COLD MORNING COFFEE

Monday morning I woke from a strange dream. My best friend, Isabel, had been sick with chicken pox and she was supposed to sing for the queen of England with these pockmarks all over her face. I remember thinking it was just like her to do something like that.

I wasn't ready to get up because I hadn't heard Mom moving around yet, so I kept my eyes closed, lying in the warm sheets, wondering about the dream. The dream reminded me of the time Isabel tried to get Jonah, a new kid in school, to notice her. That morning she painted her face — eyeliner, lipstick, rouge, mascara, everything that was supposed to make women more appealing went on. Mrs. Molina was energetically wiping Isabel's face with a tissue when I got to her house.

"See what my foolish daughter does?" she asked me. "Why does she do these things?"

I shrugged my shoulders. Of course Isabel explained it later, but at that moment I had no idea.

After a minute she gave up with the tissue and sent us on to school leaving Isabel's face looking like she had some tropical skin disease. If it had been me, I would have been so embarrassed, but Isabel just told everyone she'd gotten leprosy while working in Latin America with Mother Teresa and God would no doubt cure her before day's end.

I opened my eyes to discover I was late. I jumped up and got dressed, then headed downstairs wondering if anyone else was even up. Usually by the time I was dressed, Mom was just coming out of the bathroom. Mom and I both have the same fantastic internal clock and we've gotten it so well adjusted that neither of us ever has to be in the bathroom when the other one is — almost. Today she wasn't in the bathroom and I didn't hear her in her bedroom.

Mom opens her veterinary clinic at 9:00 a.m. She has a short commute to work: out the back door, six or seven steps across the red brick stepping stones, and into her office in the garage. Even in a downpour, she can do it without getting wet.

I got a surprise when I came downstairs. Mom was awake, or at least up. She was sitting at the kitchen table with a full coffee cup in front of her. She looked hypnotized and didn't even know I was there. I stopped at the bottom step and stared.

She was in her red plaid robe and matching slippers instead of the jeans, flannel shirt and white Reeboks she wore for work. She puts a white lab coat on when she goes out to her office. She looks good in it, like a doctor — a very pretty doctor. She's about average height, five foot five inches to my five two, slim but not skinny. Of course her most important feature is her smile. It's somehow wider than her whole face. My dad calls it her 10,000-watt smile.

〰〰 〰〰 〰〰

She wasn't smiling now and she looked like she'd been sitting there a long time. Her hair was stringy and oily and her head was resting on her arms. I couldn't tell if she was awake or asleep — and, I wasn't positive, but the coffee looked cold.

As I stepped into the kitchen she heard me and lifted her head. Her eyes met mine, but they weren't sharp and focused. It was as if she was looking at me through a rain-streaked window.

"Good morning, Margie. Why are you up so early?"

Her voice was rough like she hadn't talked to anyone since she got up.

"Mom?"

"Yes, Margie?"

I hesitated, looking away from her eyes toward the coffee cup. "Did you and Dad have a fight or something?" That was such a weird question. Mom and Dad never have that kind of fight.

She tried to laugh, but no sound came out.

"No, nothing of the sort. I don't think your dad even knows I'm up."

"How long have you been up?"

She paused and looked at the clock.

"Oh, my. You need to get off to school. I had no idea what time it was."

She started to stand up, but sat right back down, as if her legs were tied to the chair, maybe with rubber bands.

"Sweetheart, can you get your own breakfast and lunch together? There's some tuna salad from yesterday."

I looked at her closely. She knows I hate tuna.

She sighed. "Well, find something, okay?"

I nodded and got out a bowl, spoon, some granola, milk, orange juice and a cup. Then I sat down and put my finger right into Mom's coffee cup. It was as cold as the milk.

Mom nodded. "I wanted some, but I couldn't drink it."

"It didn't taste good?" I asked.

"I couldn't pick up the cup." She shook her head.

"What do you mean?"

"My hands shake, Margie." She paused. "Like Saturday night at the restaurant."

"Saturday night?"

"Yes, just like at dinner. I didn't worry about it then. I thought it was some passing thing. You know, working too hard, too much stress — that sort of thing. I'm sure it's just stress, Margie. I shouldn't be getting you worried."

I set down my spoon so gently it didn't make a sound.

I didn't think she was going to say anymore. In fact, I thought she'd fallen asleep with her eyes open, like horses sleep standing up. But she started talking again, as if I wasn't there, as if she was just thinking aloud.

"I felt okay on Sunday, just a little tired. Everything seemed fine until I lay down last night. When I closed my eyes, it was like opening them in a movie theater. There was this big Technicolor production going on with a cast of thousands and a story line I couldn't follow. I felt like I was in a Russian novel. It was exhausting. Finally I stopped trying to sleep and came down to read."

I looked around. There wasn't a book or magazine anywhere in the kitchen. "But what does it mean?"

She looked at me closely. "I don't know, Margie. Just stress, I guess. I'm going to take it easy for a little while." She paused and stared past me. "But you're going to be late. Finish your breakfast and put some lunch together. Take a candy bar if you want."

"Mom, you never let me bring candy to school."

"Of course. Just get something together for lunch and get going so you don't keep Isabel waiting."

〰〰 〰〰 〰〰

I'd never seen Mom so distracted. She is usually totally focused, even when she's doing ten things at once. She's a real in-your-face kind of parent. She wants to know what I'm doing and who I'm doing it with and why and on and on. She's usually way too overprotective and here she was sending me off to school with whatever I wanted for lunch — tuna salad, a candy bar, a can of beer. I don't think she would have noticed. I sometimes hated how overprotective she was, but this was worse.

~~~ ~~~ ~~~

In American History class that afternoon, I remember looking around like I'd never been in the room before. I was so distracted thinking about my mom. I was trying to be realistic about it. All Mom really had was shaking hands and a strange dream, but there was something else there — not what she said or did, and not the way she looked either. There was something deeper that I could feel inside.

My eyes settled on a poster in one corner of the room. It looked like a factory with those old, tall cars rolling along and men standing around putting fenders and lights on, holding screwdrivers. That's what you could see if you got up close, but from where I was sitting all you could see of the picture was a kind of ghostly image that might have been a factory. Printed over the gray were bright blue letters that read: "'History is Bunk' — Henry Ford" and over the letters was a big red circle with a line through it — "not!"

"MARGIE! Can I please have your attention up here. This is my hour, one of the few I get to spend with you during the week."

My eyes shot to the front of the room and I looked at the clock. It was 11:15, so class had only been in session five minutes and I was already in trouble.

"I'm sorry," I said, "I … I wasn't paying attention."

"Oh," Mr. Boylan sighed dramatically. "Thank you for that insight. I thought, God forbid, I might have bored you … and," he added, "with 50 minutes still remaining in the period, that would have been terrible, indeed."

I heard some giggling around the room and felt my face coloring. I nodded my head and opened the book. Isabel showed me the page number and then I looked back at Mr. Boylan.

"All right, then," he said, "now that we're all on the same page …" He paused like he was waiting for us to laugh, then shrugged. "Let's continue our investigation of the Gold Rush period — and remember we are not looking for gold. We are trying to discover the nature of the immigrant experience."

I tensed up, remembering. We'd been given an assignment to do a ten-page paper about California immigrants, and it was the last day for turning in an outline. Somehow, I'd managed to put it out of my mind. I guess preparation for my Bat Mitzvah had overwhelmed me, and my low enthusiasm for history made it easier to forget.

~~~ ~~~ ~~~

When the bell rang I'd planned to slip out of class with everyone else, but I wasn't surprised when Mr. Boylan called to me.

"Margie, if I may have a minute of your time before you leave."

I stopped halfway to the door and stood as the river of my classmates parted around me. When the last drop had run past, I went, reluctantly, to Mr. Boylan's desk. He had his grade book open and I knew he'd noticed the missing outline. Historians are too good with details.

I could hear the thunder of feet rushing down the halls and the murmur of voices. I should have been out there, rushing to my class. They only allowed four minutes from door to door and from bell to bell.

"Well, Margie, I had high hopes of turning you into a real historian this year. I guess I've failed." He made a big show of looking through the grade book. "It seems I couldn't even motivate you to complete your assignment."

I shook my head. "It's not that. I …" I said, but then I just stood there feeling foolish. I didn't have any excuse at all. I just didn't do it.

"I'm going to tell you something," Mr. Boylan said, finally. "I picked you out right at the beginning of the year."

I shook my head, not understanding. "Picked me out … for what?"

"I'm always on the lookout for a kid who will fall in love with history." Mr. Boylan said. "This year, I thought it might be you."

"Me? Why me? I don't fall in love easily."

"I don't know, Margie … it was a feeling. I was sure you were going to be the one." He paused. "In fact, I'm still sure."

"I'm not a historian, Mr. Boylan," I said uncomfortably. "I'm not even a good student in history."

"Well, maybe not this year, Margie. Maybe you're not ready. But I still think you've got it in you."

"Mr. Boylan, I couldn't even think of a topic for the report."

"You will, Margie. I'm going to help you."

He pushed the chair in under his desk and walked over to a bookshelf against the wall. He took out the teacher's edition of our history text and held it in front of him at shoulder height, one hand holding each end.

"This," he said, "is not history." He opened his hands and the book fell flat on the floor with a loud 'whack!' He pointed to it. "That is a timeline. They make me use it because the District curriculum committee picked it for all of you."

He walked over to another shelf where there was a set of encyclopedias. He pulled a book out and thumbed through it for a minute. Then he stopped and pointed to a picture of Robert E. Lee.

"Is this history?" he asked.

"I don't know … is this a trick question?" I asked.

His eyes caught mine and I looked for a smile on his face. It wasn't there.

"This!" he said, "is certainly not history. It's just facts, dehydrated and shriveled up like a used cocoon. Do you know how to recognize real history?" he asked, now looking me square in the eyes.

I shook my head. I didn't want to say anything. I hadn't ever seen Mr. Boylan get so carried away.

Mr. Boylan finally smiled.

"You can feel it," he said, "with all your senses." He took a deep breath, looking around the classroom. "It's like … it's like breathing in the richness of another time, feeling the crispness of a morning that happened a thousand years ago, smelling the salt spray of an ocean wave that crashed before you and I were born. It's seeing the exultation on the face of a mother at her child's first cries and knowing that even the child's grandchildren were gone from this earth before western civilization came into being." He sighed. "It's an incredible experience."

He turned to me, but I looked away, feeling oddly embarrassed that he'd gotten so carried away in front of me. He didn't seem embarrassed, he just looked puzzled and he stared at me without saying anything for a few seconds.

"Margie," he blurted out suddenly and he leaned over toward me as if he was about to tell me his deepest secret.

"Original sources," he whispered.

"What?" I asked.

"Original … sources," he repeated a little louder. "Find original source material. That's where real history lies — and when you find it, I'm willing to wager you'll turn into a real historian."

"Mr. Boylan …?"

"What, Margie?"

"My next class … I'm really late."

"I'll have to write you a note." He glanced up at the clock. "Oh! I'll have to write you a long note because you're quite late."

He wrote something on a page from his 'History is the Future' notepad and handed it to me.

"Don't worry, Margie. This note is accepted in as many places as American Express."

I nodded as I took the note and turned toward the door, but he wasn't quite ready to let me go.

"Margie," he said. "Find original historical sources. Stay away from the encyclopedias. Try the historical society or if you know any history buffs, ask them. Do your preliminary research and give me an outline by Tuesday after Memorial Day. You'll have this week and next, plus Memorial Day to do the major part of your research and planning. After that, all you'll have to do is the writing, but don't kill the history when you write the report. Carry it like our ancestors carried the glowing coal for the next night's fire."

"Tuesday?" I asked, trying to finish the conversation.

"Can you do it?"

"I guess I have to."

"Done then! I wish you were more enthusiastic, but I have a hunch you'll get enthusiastic when you stumble on the real thing — there's nothing like it."

"Thank you, Mr. Boylan," I said and I realized, walking down the empty hall, that Mr. Boylan had — for a time — made me stop worrying about my mother.

〰 〰 〰

Isabel gave me a curious look when I finally arrived in Algebra. After class, she stopped me in the hall and I told her the whole conversation.

"You're going to do it, aren't you?"

"I said I would, so I suppose I have to. Although I think I'd rather get a 'B' or 'C' and not have to do any work."

"You're too smart for that, Margie. Besides, I think

my mom knows a librarian who has her own collection of historical material. I haven't really done that much research yet, so maybe we can work together, you know, find some link between the person I'm writing about and the one you're writing about. It would be a lot more fun that way.

"But you've already turned in your outline."

"I'm sure Mr. Boylan wouldn't mind if I changed it. I'll ask him after school."

"Thanks," I said without feeling. "It's nice to know you're still willing to work with me even though I'm a lousy historian."

Isabel gave me a sideways look and we headed off to our next class.

< 3 >

CHANGE OF PLANS

Isabel's mother picked me up right after school to take me to my first Bat Mitzvah meeting with Rabbi Cohen. I was expecting my dad to come, but it turned out he had taken Mom to the doctor's and they hadn't told me anything about it. Isabel was staying at school to help with Teacher Appreciation Day, so Mrs. Molina took me to the meeting and picked me up afterward to drop me off at home.

My folks hadn't returned from the doctor's yet, so Mrs. Molina brought me home with her. Isabel met us at the car and she and I helped unload the groceries. While we were putting stuff in the refrigerator, Isabel told me my dad had called. They were running late at the doctor's. He wanted me to have dinner with the Molinas and my Mom gave Isabel instructions for me to check in on a Persian cat staying in mom's clinic. Isabel and I walked back to my house while Mrs. Molina was making enchiladas.

On the way Isabel started talking about Jonah. He wasn't in classes with either of us, but going in and out of classes, we'd had a chance to see him. Isabel even bumped into him once coming out of English class. She was so excited to tell me about it. It was embarrassing. She was acting like a kindergartner and, worse, I was jealous.

"Well, I guess you're an older woman now," Isabel said as we crossed Ashby Avenue. Her eyes were sparkling and I knew something was coming.

"What do you mean?"

"Your birthday, Swifty."

"I know that, Isabel. I'm thirteen, so what?"

"Margie. I'm talking about Jonah ... I'll bet he likes older women. I probably haven't got a chance now that you're a grown woman with me still a naive girl of twelve point eight years."

"Right ... I'm sure he'll notice the difference immediately," I said in my best sarcastic tones. "I certainly feel a lot more mature. In fact, I'm not sure I'm going to allow you to hang with me anymore."

Isabel looked me over appraisingly, looking for the sure signs of my emerging feminine maturity. There weren't any, at least not any new ones since my birthday on Saturday. Isabel had kept her silence as she looked at me, but I couldn't stand the suspense any longer.

"You're thinking again, Isabel. You can't hide it from me."

"As a matter of fact ..." Her voice was quiet, thoughtful. I didn't like it.

I waited for a couple more seconds, watching for some hint of what she was up to.

"Isabel?"

"Uh, huh."

"What's going on?"

"I don't want to talk about Jonah anymore."

"Okay ... What are you working on in art class?"

"No, Margie. What I mean is that I want to talk about why I don't want to talk about Jonah."

"What?" I asked. "I didn't follow that. Why don't you want to talk about Jonah?"

She hesitated. "Because I really like him."

"So do I — at least I think I do. Isn't that a good reason to talk about him?"

"No!" she said, stopping suddenly right at the foot of the Elmwood branch library steps. I stopped, too, which meant the family coming down the stair had to part around us like the Red Sea.

"Because I don't want Jonah to come between us," she said.

Then I was silent. I'd never thought our game about Jonah would ever be more than a game. With so little experience with any kind of friends, I couldn't imagine having a boyfriend.

"Could that really happen?" I asked.

"You know it could, Margie." She said it as if I ought to know, without a doubt.

"But I *don't* know."

"Well you should. That's the way the world works. All the really good relationships between women are eventually ruined by some stupid man — or stupid boy in our case. In the end, both women realize the boy isn't worth it and they go on to other things, but their relationship is ruined forever. I don't want that to happen to us."

I didn't say anything right away. It was such a strange idea.

"But that wouldn't happen unless …"

"Unless what?" Isabel asked.

"Unless …" I started laughing, "unless one of us actually talked to Jonah."

Isabel laughed. "That's true. Well I won't talk to him, if you won't."

"It's a deal."

～～～ ～～～ ～～～

Even before we got the door unlocked, I heard Skittle mewing. I let her out of the cage and Isabel and I played with her a while. Then Isabel kept her company while I checked the answering machine. There was a message from the Rabbi. He wanted to check in with me about my mother. He realized how worried I was about her and wanted to talk about it. He also had an idea for my Bat Mitzvah speech.

At the moment, learning Hebrew didn't seem very important and learning my Torah portion was just another history assignment. "How fair are your tents, Oh Jacob ..." Maybe it was poetic or even profound, but with my mom sick and everything else going on, I had a hard time caring about 'fair tents.'

Back in the clinic, Isabel helped me put some fresh food and water in Skittle's cage. Then I put her in for the night. She mewed miserably, but we said 'good-bye.' I locked up the office and we headed back to Isabel's for dinner.

∿∿ ∿∿ ∿∿

Mrs. Molina met us at the door, smiling. "Dinner's almost ready, senoritas. Isabel, you go in and wash up. I would like to talk to my other daughter."

"Yes, Mom?" I said, smiling.

"About your Rabbi," she said, looking at me, "I hope he doesn't mind working with a Bat Mitzvah girl who is part Catholic."

I would have denied being Catholic with anyone else, but the truth was I felt so much at home with Isabel's family that being Catholic didn't really seem strange at all.

∿∿ ∿∿ ∿∿

Isabel was my first, real, long lasting friend. Up until I met her, my friends were kids who moved away, or who lived too far away to see often, or went to the same pre-school but went on to a different kindergarten, or kids who didn't like me or I didn't like. I ended up quite a loner.

As I got older, I found I liked being on my own a lot of the time, but it was harder when I was young. I saw other girls who had sisters and I was so jealous. For most of two years, I demanded that Mom give me a baby sister — either older or younger, it didn't matter. She had several different responses but they all meant the same thing, "no." It wasn't until she asked how I would feel about having a little brother that I realized the real risk with babies — you never knew what you'd get.

Mom tried hard to find friends, peers and playmates for me. She was always making plans to get me together with other kids my age. On a Saturday morning or a weekday afternoon she would say, "let's go visit your friend Sarah" or "let's have a picnic with Katie and Alexandra" and we would go on carefully planned outings. I didn't realize then how much effort she put into my social life — but it didn't work. I don't think you can make friends with "play dates." What I needed was a neighborhood kid wandering down the sidewalk, turning up my walk, knocking on my door and saying, "Can Margie come out and play?" "Yes," I would have said, "yes."

Then, when I figured I would always be a loner, Isabel came along. Isabel isn't at all like me. She's also an only child and we're the same age, but everything else is different. I'm blonde with wavy hair and she has curly, black hair. I'm tall and gawky and she's short and very pretty and, of course, there's the Jewish-Catholic thing.

Her parents, like mine, have never been divorced. She refers to them as "the original equipment." Where most kids say "mom and dad" or "the folks" Isabel always says "the original equipment." I got so used to hearing it, I was surprised when anyone reacted to it.

Isabel moved into our neighborhood, just a block away, in the summer before sixth grade, but she was on the other side of Ashby Avenue, a busy street, and I didn't know she was there even after school started. We were in different classes and though we passed each other in the halls, masses of kids passed through the halls. Most of us stuck with our own crowd. By that time, I was part of a group of girls, but still working on developing close friendships.

I finally met Isabel, officially, at Cedar Rose Park. The San Francisco Mime Troupe was doing a performance of ... something or other. I don't remember what, maybe 'The Great Air Robbery.' Anyway, I was sitting with a small group of kids from school. As usual, I was at the edge of the group, sort of included, but not really. I was glad to be there in that uncomfortable kind of way, not sure what the other kids thought of me and wanting really badly not to care.

One of the performers was playing a trumpet next to the stage and there was a long, loud, drumbeat: boom, boom, boom. Suddenly I saw Isabel, sitting about twenty feet to the side with her head turned toward me. She saw me and nodded quickly. Then she turned back to look at the stage. When I looked over a couple minutes later, leaning forward to see around a pair of blue jeans standing beside me, she was gone. I was surprised she'd disappeared so quickly, then doubly surprised when the blue jeans leaned over and spoke to me.

"Enjoying the show?" Isabel asked loudly over the drumbeat.

I jerked away, startled. Then I quickly recovered and smiled at her.

She stood quietly, watching the show. Then she leaned over again.

"You're Jewish, aren't you?"

I'd intended to ask her if she wanted to sit down, but her question didn't seem like a great start for a friendship. I'm proud I'm Jewish, but when someone says "you're Jewish," it usually isn't a friendly opener.

I waited a second before answering. "Yeah?" I said, sort of like "so what?"

She sat down beside me. "Me too."

I hesitated. I'd seen her in the hallways, joking with other girls and even flirting with some of the boys. She seemed nice enough, but she sure wasn't Jewish. For one thing, Jews don't wear crosses.

"So?" she said.

"So what?"

"So what's your name?"

I turned to look at her, expecting a cold look like I'd seen before at the school. But that's not what I saw. She looked friendly — and I couldn't fit it all together.

"That's okay, you don't have to tell me." Her voice was quieter now that the drumming had stopped. "My name is Isabel Molina and yours is Marjorie Belzer, known as 'Margie' to your friends."

I think I must have looked surprised or something.

"And you live on Hillegass Street ..."

I nodded, wondering how she knew.

"3033 Hillegass?"

"How do you know so much about me?" I said, sharply.

"We're neighbors."

"We are?"

"Yes, I live on Hillegass, too, just across Ashby. I was hoping we'd meet. I thought we might be able to walk to school together — or something."

"Are you really Jewish?" I asked.

She grinned at me.

"Yeah, right." She paused. "Actually I'm Catholic from my socks all the way up to my crucifix. I guess that leaves my head out. The original equipment, you know, my parents, are from Mexico. Very Catholic down there — rosa, rosa, rosary."

We became instant friends and, despite what she said about leaving her head out, Isabel was very Catholic just like I was very Jewish and, surprisingly, that worked out just fine. Even my original equipment, who would never let me walk to school alone seemed very comfortable with me walking to school with Isabel. They figured out right away what I just got a glimpse of that day — Isabel was a special kid. So my parents adopted Isabel into our family just like the Molinas adopted me into theirs and I went from having no close friends to having a friend who was as close as a sister, maybe closer.

~~~ ~~~ ~~~

Mr. Molina excused himself after dinner to do something and Isabel told her mother about the report I had to do. Mrs. Molina was excited for me, much more excited than I was. She was a big California history buff, particularly the history of the Spanish in California. She told us about a friend of hers, Victoria Snyder, who was the caretaker for a collection of old books and newspapers and a lot of other California historical stuff.

"Victoria Snyder," she said in a faraway voice. "We worked to put that collection together when she was a librarian at the UC Berkeley Library. I was just a student, but I had a work-study assignment in the library and she got me involved in this big project."

"I didn't know you did that, mom," Isabel said.

Mrs. Molina turned to us like she'd forgotten we were there. "Maybe," she said, smiling, "there are one or two things about me I haven't told you yet."

"Were you a librarian?"

"No. You need a college degree to be a librarian. I was just a student."

"What did you do?" I asked.

"It was a big project," she answered. "We called people all over California: historical societies, chambers of commerce, individuals, libraries. We asked people to donate whatever they had to create this special California historical collection."

"And people were willing to give their own books and stuff to the library?" Isabel asked. "Why would they do that?"

"First of all we promised a safe environment for the books and we promised donors they would get credit for their donations — including tax deductions. We didn't get everything we asked for and there were several special documents we really worked hard for, but the owners wouldn't give them up. We did get many good books and manuscripts and we got some real odds and ends: a carved wooden bedpost, a piece of a quilt, a miner's lamp. Interesting things, but not materials for a library.

"UC Berkeley set up a temporary room for the books while the new room was being constructed — but the new room never happened."

"Why not?"

"I think it had to do with Proposition 13 and all the services that were being cut. I just remember Victoria saying the university couldn't afford to build the new room and we had to figure out what to do with the materials. That's how they ended up in Victoria's home. Some of the major donors formed a donor committee and asked for the materials back, insisting the University hadn't met its obligation.

"It seemed like everything we'd done was going to be wasted. Then Victoria proposed that she would set up a collection room in her home to meet the donor requirements and keep them there until the University provided the room they had promised. I remember the day she drove off with the last load of materials in her Volkswagen van."

"She still has them?" Isabel asked.

Mrs. Molina nodded. "The last I heard, she was still negotiating with the University."

After dessert, Isabel and I talked more about our reports, and how we could make them come alive for Mr. Boylan. I reluctantly agreed to sacrifice my Saturday and give Mrs. Snyder's collection a try.

Mom was there, smiling for me when I got home from Isabel's. From her expression, I figured she'd passed the doctor's examination with flying colors and my spirits soared for a moment. Then I looked at my dad's face. The tension around his eyes and the grim line of his mouth told a different story. Mom was really sick.

Yet, when they told me what the doctor said, it didn't seem so bad. I mean the words: "flu-like symptoms," "nervous condition," and even "unknown causes," didn't sound that terrible. What scared me was Mom, the idea that she needed to smile at me when it was obvious she didn't feel like smiling at all.

Mom got up Tuesday morning to see me off to school. She smiled at me, cooked me oatmeal and even sat with me while I ate. She seemed much better, like she was getting over it. She let me do the talking and it almost seemed normal.

"Margie," she said, looking past me to the window, "how's the work coming on your Bat Mitzvah portion? I haven't heard you chanting any Hebrew for a while."

I waited until she turned to face me. Even then, I didn't answer. She looked at me quietly, as if she was reading my mind.

"You're worried about me," she said, her voice soothing and calm.

I nodded and waited for her to tell me I shouldn't be worried — but she didn't. Instead, she smiled.

"You're my daughter. You're supposed to worry about me."

I looked at her closely. Was she kidding?

"I'm thirteen years old," I said finally, "what good does my worrying do?"

That's when she laughed, full and unselfconscious. For a moment, I saw her as she'd been before she got sick and I felt better, more confident that things would turn out all right.

"What good does anyone's worrying do?" she asked.

"Worrying just takes energy away from what we need to do." She paused, staring at me. "But not worrying is a little like not breathing — you can't do it for very long. And, worrying does show that you care."

As she said that, I could feel her sickness again and I wanted to put that off. I wanted more of her smile and her laugh. I wanted her to talk about something that had nothing to do with being sick.

"Mom, tell me about your Bat Mitzvah."

"I already told you. My Torah portion was big on punishments, specifically the punishments for stealing, infidelity, lying, disrespect for parents." She put special emphasis on disrespect for parents. "There was a lot about stoning, as I recall," she added with a teasing smile.

"But wait a minute," I said with a completely bewildered expression pasted on my face. "Sandra from my Hebrew class got that portion for her Bat Mitzvah. Do they still use the same Torah they used way back when you were a kid?"

"Margie, that's …" She stared at me in confusion. Then she burst into laughter. "You tricked me, Margie."

I pointed at her like "gotcha" and started laughing. She joined in.

"What about your Bat Mitzvah service? How did you feel when you walked out in front of all those people?"

"Scared, Margie. I was shaking in my boots. I forgot to breathe and nearly tripped on my own feet as I walked to the bima. I caught myself, and managed to stay upright, but I didn't have anyone in the congregation fooled. Boy did I get kidded about that little display of grace!"

"How was your speech?"

"It was fine, Margie. For years, when I thought about it, I rewrote it in my mind, substituting clever phrases and well thought-out ideas for what I had already said. The new ideas seemed so much wittier and more profound. I felt like it had been my moment in the spotlight and I'd blown it. Now I look back and think that it was exactly the right speech for me as I was then. I couldn't have done better even if I'd been able to stop my voice from quaking. If I'd said those things I planned afterwards, it would have been awful."

She gave me a probing look. "Are you worried about the speech, Margie?"

I nodded "I haven't spoken in public much."

"I know," she said. Then she paused, thinking. "It seems like you have so much to worry about these days." She reached out and touched my hair. It was the softest of sensations and I held still, not wanting her to stop.

"So what do I do, Mom?"

"What you do is practice and prepare until you know exactly what you want to say."

"And that's it? Then it comes easily?"

She shook her head. "No, I don't think speaking in public ever comes easily. It certainly hasn't for me."

"But then …"

"Margie, when the time comes you'll either be able to get up and give your prepared speech or you won't. If you can't, go up to the bima and start speaking. If you've studied well, you'll be able to complete a speech even if it's not what you planned. It might even be better. The most important thing is to make sure you are there, all of you, your thoughts, your fears, your emotions, all right there. Then you tap into them and give your speech — and whatever you do will be perfect."

"Really, Mom?"

She looked me in the eyes. "Believe in yourself, Margie. I know you'll make all of us proud."

I suddenly noticed the clock. I was already five minutes later than I usually left for school. I knew Isabel would be waiting for me, wondering where I was. As I stood up the phone rang. We both knew it was Isabel.

"Go ahead, Margie, I'll tell her you're on your way."

I nodded my head. "See you tonight."

I grabbed my backpack and some fruit and dashed

out the back door. As I walked past the kitchen window I saw Mom sitting at the table, holding the phone, looking at me — or at least in my direction. I waved, but she didn't see me, didn't wave back. I hesitated, watching as she set the phone down, leaned forward in her chair and covered her face in her hands.

~~~ ~~~ ~~~

Dinner that night seemed better. Mom and Dad smiled and talked small talk. It felt pretty much like normal — except Mom went to bed right after dinner and Dad spent the rest of the evening in the living room in the dark with his hands folded motionless in his lap. I missed the light of his drafting table and the scratching sound of his sharp pencil drawing rafters or sketching floor plans. I sat in the kitchen taking notes on a short story I was reading for school, feeling as if I was alone in the house.

~~~ ~~~ ~~~

Wednesday morning I was on my own. Dad finally got up, red-eyed and mumbling, to see me to the door. He told me Mom was sleeping in. I didn't ask him why he wasn't getting ready for work, or what was happening with his big construction project. I didn't ask him anything.

At 11:15, I got called to the school office.

Mrs. Snow was sitting, staring at a stack of forms in front of her, looking distracted. She glanced up as I stepped to the counter, then looked at me blankly for a minute.

"Oh, Marjorie. Your dad called. He said you should go home with Isabel Molina after school."

"Why?" I asked.

She shrugged her shoulders. "Something about your mother, I think."

~~~ ~~~ ~~~

When we got to Isabel's that afternoon, Mrs. Molina told me my mom and dad were at the hospital. Mom was getting a CBC, which Mrs. Molina explained was a complete blood count. The idea of counting blood seemed funny to me, whether you counted all the blood or just some of it, but my mom being in the hospital was not funny. Dad called after dinner while Isabel and I were cutting up melon and washing blueberries for dessert. I popped a blueberry in my mouth and picked up the phone. Dad suggested I spend the night at Isabel's.

"What's wrong Dad?"

"Nothing, Margie."

"But why don't you want me home? What's wrong with Mom?"

"It's not that, Margie. We're both just really tired out from running around to doctors. We thought you'd rather stay with the Molinas than hang around with us. We're not planning on jumping out of bed early in the morning or anything. You know Mom doesn't get sick much and she's trying to get as much mileage out of it as she can, sleeping in, getting me to play nursemaid — the whole thing."

"Sure, Dad. I'll stay here, but I hope Isabel's family doesn't get tired of me."

"I don't think there's much chance of that."

\~\~\~ \~\~\~ \~\~\~

Thursday morning, Isabel and I got out of the house ten minutes early and walked to my house. I wanted to see my folks before starting another day of school. I wanted to say good morning, get a hug — get the day off to a good start. I unlocked the kitchen door and Isabel waited outside.

The house was like a tomb, dark and far too quiet, but I knew they were there. I could feel it. I tiptoed up the stairs, passing my room on the way. The door to their room was half open and I looked in.

Mom was in bed, asleep. The curtains were still drawn and Dad was sitting in the big brown, overstuffed chair, also asleep. I stared at them for a minute. I thought about waking Dad up, but I was confused. I couldn't make any sense out of what I saw. I walked over to the bed and kissed Mom on the forehead as she'd done to me for the past thousand years. Then I kissed Dad on the head and left. He murmured something as I was heading down the stairs, but I just went out and locked the kitchen door behind me.

"They're sleeping in today," I said, casually, looking away from Isabel.

～～ ～～ ～～

There was another call for me at school. This one came early in the morning, while Ms. DeLeon was teaching us to conjugate Spanish verbs. The message was much the same. "Go home with Isabel Molina." Again there were no details and, again, when we got to Isabel's house Mrs. Molina had more information from my dad.

"The tests were 'inconclusive,'" she said. The hospital had made a referral to a neurologist at the Center for Treatment of Infectious Diseases in Palo Alto. That's where my mom and dad were. They wouldn't be back until Saturday afternoon.

"What's going on?" I asked. I was facing Mrs. Molina, but I was asking the universe.

She shook her head. "Margie, dear child," she said, "God is watching out for your mother."

My eyes fell to the crucifix around her neck and I fingered the Star of David I wore. They were just jewelry. If God knew my mom was sick, He sure wasn't in a hurry to do anything about it.

～～ ～～ ～～

The phone rang as I was getting ready for bed. I hoped it would be Mom, so I didn't put the toothbrush in my mouth, anticipating someone would call me to the phone. When no one called my name, I started in on my teeth, and then Mr. Molina called me to the phone. It was my mom.

"Margie," she said, "how are you?"

"I'm okay, Mom," I said, swallowing the toothpaste. "Are you at the hospital now?"

"No. They aren't quite ready to check me in yet so we got a room in a B&B, a bed and breakfast. It's very comfortable and you should see what they serve for breakfast. I think I'd really enjoy it if I were here for a different purpose — and if I were hungry." She paused. It sounded like she was catching her breath. Then she continued. "As it is, all I can look forward to is getting up early in the morning, skipping breakfast and showing up at the raw end of the morning to get perforated by the doctors." Her voice trailed off.

"Are you getting better, Mom?"

"Just a second, Margie. Your dad came back in."

I heard her talking to Dad and heard his voice for a minute, then she came back on the line.

"He was asking our hosts if we could get breakfast after the tests tomorrow morning. By the time we get back from the hospital, there's no breakfast." She hesitated. "That way your dad could eat. It doesn't matter much to me. I don't get very hungry."

"What is it, Mom? What's wrong with you?" That seemed like a stupid question, but I meant it. I suddenly felt like Mom should know, not as if she was holding out on us, but like she just hadn't given it enough thought.

"I don't know, Margie. It seems so strange that with all the doctors I've seen and all these dreadful tests, everyone is still asking the same questions."

"But don't you know?"

"Of course not, Margie. What do you mean?"

"I'm not sure, Mom … but I feel like … like maybe somewhere inside you know something … I don't mean consciously … more like a lost memory of something." I stopped, hearing how foolish I sounded. "I'm sorry. I'm not making any sense, am I?"

"No, Margie, you are making sense. I've been thinking the same thing." She paused again. Then she continued in an airy voice as if out of breath. "Sometimes I think it's a mystery and I have all the clues, or at least all the information. But now I don't have much energy." Another pause. "I can't think as clearly as before, Margie. It seems like deep down inside somewhere I really do know or should know why this is happening to me, but it never is more than a fleeting impression, gone as soon as I notice it."

She was silent then and I didn't know what to say, or even what I was thinking. "Margie, we'll be home on Saturday. We can talk about everything then. I'm sure we'll have an answer." There was a long pause. "With all the tests they've done, they'd better have something by then."

I had trouble sleeping that night. My head was spinning. I kept asking myself what I could do.

∿∿∿ ∿∿∿ ∿∿∿

Isabel and I were talking about our history reports while she was setting the table for dinner. We were both getting more excited about going to Mrs. Snyder's personal library which Isabel had started calling the Purloined Letters Collection. In the middle of one of Isabel's sentences, it struck me that it was Friday, Shabbat. Suddenly I wanted the comfort of the Shabbat ritual with my family. I'd been away from home so long I was beginning to feel like a refugee.

I asked Isabel for two candles — all she could find were those little short ones that looked more Catholic than Jewish, I think they're called votive candles — and

I did my own Shabbat with a napkin covering my head. I sang the blessings alone and then joined the Molinas for dinner.

I barely slept that night and when I did, I had dreams like those my mom described — in Technicolor with thousands of characters. In the dreams, I was searching for something. I felt I was constantly getting closer to an answer, but I never reached it.

< 4 >

AN APPOINTMENT WITH HISTORY

Isabel and I spent Saturday morning discussing my report. After lunch, we got on an AC Transit bus headed into Oakland for our appointment with history. We had to transfer once and walk two blocks to get to Mrs. Snyder's.

We stood at the foot of the stairs leading to an old Victorian house. The stairs were steep and the house was narrow and tall. It seemed to lean over as if it would fall across the street and crush Isabel and me under a pile of old rubble. In my mind, I saw the headlines: "Two Teenage Girls Killed Under the Weight of History."

Paint was peeling from the shingles and the window frames were cracked and discolored. A dead patch of garden in front and the bare branches of an equally dead tree made it all look more disturbing. I squinted, looking up at a window hiding in the shadows of the overhanging roof. I was sure no one was up there looking down on us — at least pretty sure.

"Wow!" Isabel said. "I knew this was Mrs. Snyder's house, but I still keep thinking 'library' and this doesn't look like one. I think I like my libraries to look a little more like … like libraries, I guess."

"Are you nervous about the house?" I asked, laughing.

"Of course not," she said, sharply.

"Then let's go in."

She hesitated, then started up the stairs. "Okay, but afterwards I want you to buy me an ice cream cone at the parlor we passed."

"All right," I said, following her up the stairs. "It's a deal."

As we reached a landing, the door suddenly opened and a pretty girl, maybe eight years old, came out with a jump rope. She had Goldilocks hair and freckles and looked like she'd stepped out of the past. She came down the stairs, looking at Isabel, then me.

"Well, go up," she said. "My grandma is waiting for you." Then, noticing our hesitation she joined us in looking up at the house.

"Don't keep her waiting," she said. Then she bounced down the rest of the stairs and started skipping rope down the sidewalk.

We turned and headed up the stairs, but the door opened again just as we reached the top. In the open doorway stood a very elegant, older woman, tall and thin, with her hair cut in an almost boyish style. Her face was narrow and serious, but as she motioned us through the door, she smiled, her gray eyebrows arching upward.

∿∿∿ ∿∿∿ ∿∿∿

I immediately loved the house. I'd only been in a couple of Victorian houses, but the feel of the tall narrow hallways and the high, decorated ceilings was really cool. The windows were covered with heavy drapes tied back to let in a small amount of light. The living room was full of upholstered furniture, faded and worn at the edges, and wood furniture that was polished smooth from years of use. There were photographs and paintings all around the walls. Each had an index card tucked into the frame with the date of the picture, the photographer and the place the picture was taken. There was a scene of downtown Oakland, where Telegraph Avenue runs into Broadway, from sometime in the late 1800s. I've been there and it's nothing like it was then. There were houses, neat old classic houses kind of like Mrs. Snyder's, right on Telegraph Avenue. I wondered if the photographs had been donated with the historical documents.

Another photograph showed a family all dressed up in their Sunday best. The clothes were beautiful, but the expressions on the family's faces were so serious. I guess back then people didn't say "cheese."

Next to it was a painting of a California mission at sunset done by someone with a Mexican-sounding name. As I was moving on to look at another picture, showing Berkeley right after the 1906 earthquake, I heard Mrs. Snyder clear her throat.

"Girls," she said, "welcome to my home."

At that moment I realized that, while I'd been checking out the pictures, Mrs. Snyder had been checking us out. Looking at her more closely, I thought she seemed too old to have been a librarian when Mrs. Molina was going to college.

"This is just the house," she said, her voice cracking as if she hadn't spoken in months — or maybe years. "It's a classic old house, but it's not history. The manuscripts are in the library, upstairs." She led us out of the living room and, haltingly, up some stairs that ended in a dark hallway.

She walked slowly down the hall, clearly tired from the climb.

"It gets harder and harder to visit my old friends up here," she said, breathing heavily.

Isabel tugged on my shirtsleeve and pulled me back. She had one of her "looks" as if she'd been letting her imagination run a little too freely again.

"What if she locks us up in a closet and never lets us out?" she whispered, faking a shiver of fear.

I smiled. While I could see she was playing, I could also see she was talking herself into being spooked. I decided to play along.

"I don't know," I said, frowning. "Do you think she might? Could she?"

Isabel nodded seriously and I nodded right back at her.

"What if she cooks us up and eats us like in *Hansel and Gretel*?" I asked, my eyes wide and my mouth dropping open.

Isabel smiled briefly, but Mrs. Snyder had stopped and turned — and I knew she'd heard.

"Don't worry, girls," she said. "I'm a vegetarian."

We glanced at each other, then down at the floor. Her hearing was still good, that's for sure. After a second, she turned and continued down the hall.

The hallway ended abruptly at a door that clearly didn't belong in the house. It was new and plain and seemed more substantial than the decorative doors we'd seen everywhere else. Our shadows followed us until the darkness swallowed them. Mrs. Snyder swung the door open and held it for us. Beyond it the hallway continued and the air was suddenly cold.

"You'll get used to the temperature," she said, reading my thoughts.

She led us down the hallway past two closed doors. She opened the third and last door and turned on the light switch. Inside the small room were floor-to-ceiling bookshelves arranged in narrow rows.

"These are first-person manuscripts; diaries, journals, autobiographies. All of them are unpublished, there are no copies anywhere in the world," she said. "Now that's something to think about. This is real history, one of a kind. Handle it with care."

We stepped into the room and looked around. Even

with the lights on the room was shadowy and cold. Thick curtains covered the windows. Mrs. Snyder saw me peering into the darkness.

"Sunlight is hard on old documents. The paper becomes brittle and the ink fades. I try to keep the room as dark as I can." I nodded and shivered with the cold. "Same with the cool air. Cool, dry air is the best."

She pointed to two shelves. "Check those."

"But how do you know what we're looking for?" Isabel asked.

Mrs. Snyder smiled. "Your mother told me, Isabel."

"Those are turn-of-the-century documents from the top shelf to the bottom." She turned to the door. "Call if you need help." I looked around, then turned to thank her, but she was gone, leaving me wondering how she was suddenly able to move so fast.

"That is one strange lady," Isabel said. "How did she know I was Isabel?"

I gave her a "duh" look, and pointed to her hair and then mine. "She knows your mother."

The "books" were all different sizes and shapes. Some were bound in leather, some were loose pages in boxes. I picked up a loose stack of papers and carefully carried it to a small stand where I could look at it. When I looked back for Isabel, I couldn't see her.

"Isabel?"

There was no answer.

"Isabel!"

"Margie, I'm right here."

She was standing just a few feet away, half hidden by a tall bookshelf and the shadows.

"Why didn't you answer?"

"I was reading. I found a neat book about a stamp collector ... from Germany. His name was Helmut Briones and he was a new immigrant. This could make a really cool report."

I let her go back to her reading and lifted the first

page off the top of a stack of papers. It was a diary by a Chinese herbalist named Lee Chau Wing who treated farm animals somewhere in California during the 1890s. I was quickly drawn into it. Mostly I found myself comparing what I knew from my mom about modern veterinarians to the things he described. I tried to imagine how I could tell Mr. Lee's life in a report. How had a Chinese doctor become a healer of animals in a new country? I thought it would make a great report.

The diary was full of details about Mr. Lee's life. I guess he must have been working hard to learn English or he would have written in Chinese.

In an entry dated June 14, he described a kind of plague that was killing cattle:

June 14: Like last year, cattle are sick. There is something not in the soil they need. I speak to others who work with cattle but they do not know about this. In last year, we gave them alfalfa from along the creek. They did better then. This year the creek is dry and no alfalfa grows. We will try to move cattle before they become weak. Maybe closer to water soil will be different and they will get what they need from the grasses.

There were several entries telling about the days they spent moving the cattle to a place far away from the farm where different grasses grew. Then he wrote this entry:

June 28: The cattle doing much better now. Many died before we moved them and others died while we were moving, but the ones who made the long trip doing much better now. New calves are doing well, but it is hard to keep them together so far from the farm. Some keep running off and I have been steady working to keep the herd from wandering away.

By early July, Mr. Lee reported that the rains had started again and he described bringing the cattle back to the farm:

July 26: We are back now and things okay. Last night we brought the cattle back to the pasture. Storm came up about five miles from farm and rain so hard we couldn't see. We tried to stop, but cows were spooked by lightning and best thing seemed to be to keep them running in right direction. Almost midnight when we got them back to farm. Storm over then and cows happy to be home.

I stayed at the farmhouse because it was late and the rain and wind so strong. When we got to house, everyone was up and running around. Earlier, one of boys heard scratching at the door and opened it to a wet raccoon who rushed into the living room and disappeared behind the couch. When we came in, the boys were running around trying to trap the raccoon. For some while, I just sat and laughed.

I finally caught raccoon in towel and put outside. I got scratched, but so tired I didn't notice until morning. I cleaned and put poultice on it but it still hurts.

As I read the entry, I thought about the stories my mother told me about working with animals. Berkeley has lots of wild animals because of the parks around. Tilden Park, in the Berkeley hills, has all kinds of animals, not bears or mountain lions, but bobcats, deer, feral cats (those are house cats that have gone wild). The raccoons in Berkeley live under houses and in bushes — close to people. Mom has treated several pets after fights with raccoons. They're bold, my mom told me, not afraid of anything. Sometimes they get into houses through cat doors and eat the cat's food while the poor cat watches and hisses.

~~~ ~~~ ~~~

Isabel had been very quiet and I looked to see what she was doing. She had her little pocket notebook out and was writing furiously. I didn't interrupt her. I was pretty involved in my own reading. In the next several entries Mr. Lee visited a few other farms and looked in on some new calves and lambs. He even did something or other with chickens. It was funny to think about. I tried to imagine my mother peering into the beak of a chicken, but I kept seeing a turkey baster and a carving knife.

Then, as the summer of 1894 turned into fall, something began changing in the diary. Mr. Lee's writing, so careful and neat before, became difficult to read, but I struggled to make it out. In my mind, I was starting to develop an outline for the report. I hoped I would be able to integrate my ideas with whatever Isabel was working on, but for the moment, all I wanted was to see what would happen next. I had to keep reminding myself that I was reading about a real person. It seemed too intense, too real, to be history.

It was in early August when Mr. Lee first reported that he was sick. By August 20, he was clearly worried and it started me thinking about my mother:

August 20: Pain is in my head much of the time. When I sleep it becomes better, but eyes are tired and ears ring constantly. I have asked my son to come help. He has studied some medicine and maybe can help. He is a good son. I no longer leave my small house. Mr. Patterson sends boys over to bring me things. I am so frustrating. I help the animals and cannot help myself. I fear that I have small time left.

August 25: At last, Yang is here. Shaking is too much. No longer can I control my hands.

I set down the page and looked around. I didn't know where I was. Then I saw Isabel bent over a table nearby. In my bones, I knew Mr. Lee had died just after completing the August 25 entry. There was more to the diary but it was obvious the later entries had been written by Mr. Lee's son. I didn't read them right away, my mind was strug-

gling to accept the fact that I had just witnessed someone's death, a death that happened almost 100 years ago.

I hesitated, then picked up the next page of the diary
and started to read the son's entries. The writing was
smooth again and the grammar was more polished than
the father's had been:

*September 2: I brought father today to Stockton for burial.
It was very hard for me, loading his body onto the old
cart and hitching up Gladys. She understood our awful
errand and refused to pull at first, but I was patient
with her and explained as if she were a child and she
seemed to understand.*

*Took two days to get to Stockton on rutted roads. I fought
to keep dignity as I drove even though no one was there
to observe. Hard to keep from crying. My father had been
a good and noble man and he had taught me so much.*

*September 3: Today we said good-bye to father. My sister
Lin Sun was there with her three daughters. The girls
cried the hardest. They did not know their grandfather
so well, but my sister had taught them to respect and love
him anyway.*

*Late on this night, I talked to my sister about father's
illness, about the diary and the things he told me before
he died. I asked if she would give me her permission to …*

"Girls?"

I looked up and saw that Mrs. Snyder had returned.
Isabel's face looked as if she had just gotten off an
airplane and wasn't sure where she she'd landed. I felt
the same way. I had never found history to be anything
like this before. This was clearly what Mr. Boylan meant
when he spoke about "real history."

"I have to close up now." Mrs. Snyder's voice was
breathy from walking up the stairs. "I trust you've found
something useful."

"Oh, we have. I mean I have," Isabel blurted. "Did you, Margie?"

"Yes," I said. "This was wonderful. Except I felt sad about Mr. Lee."

"Who?" Mrs. Snyder asked.

"Mr. Lee ... oh, never mind," realizing she probably wouldn't know who I was talking about.

"Can we come back tomorrow?" Isabel asked.

Mrs. Snyder shook her head slowly. "No. I wish you could, but I'm going to Sacramento tomorrow. There's a meeting of the Association of Amateur California Historians. It will keep me until late in the day and I'm staying over. I'll be coming back early on Monday. Weren't you able to get what you wanted?"

Isabel looked at me for a second. "Well," she said, "I've made a few notes and I think I have some good starting material for a report, but ... "

I shrugged my shoulders. "We were hoping to get all our research done, and then we were going to figure out how to link our reports." I paused. "I suppose we can work something out."

"Well, I do hope so. I should have said something about going away, but I just thought you needed a little inspiration. I guess I made a wrong assumption and now I'm afraid I might not have helped you at all."

"Oh no, Mrs. Snyder. You've helped us tremendously. If we need to, we can always go to the library and get some more general stuff. It's just that we got so wrapped up in the books."

I took a deep breath. "Mrs. Snyder, is it possible I could take a book ...?"

"Home?" she asked, finishing the sentence for me. "Dear child, I never let anyone take anything from this room. I'm sorry. These books were entrusted to me and I take that very seriously."

I hesitated. "It's just that I ... I mean it was so ..." I was stuttering, not knowing what to say, wishing I hadn't said anything at all.

"No. I'm sorry. It can't be done. No."

"I shouldn't have asked." I said quickly. "It's just that the diary I was reading was so amazing."

"The documents are wonderful, aren't they? How about this? Why don't you take another ten minutes and you can talk and see where you are. I'm afraid that's the best I can do, though. I have an appointment this evening."

After she left, Isabel and I started talking. Soon a plan emerged for a report that would be based on an imaginary meeting between Lee Yang and Mr. Briones in January of 1894 on the road to Mr. Lee's house. I needed to finish the last few pages of the diary. I picked them up:

Late on this night, I talked to my sister about father's illness, about the diary and things he told me before he died. I asked if she would give me her permission to examine his body. I have made some study of the body, both from Chinese and English texts, and I read of the great English doctor named Bright who did autopsies to determine cause of death. I know no American doctor who would do an autopsy on a Chinese, and I have a thought as to what might have killed him. "If we do not learn from things, they will happen again," I told her. She only turned away. She did not need to tell me about respect for ancestors.

Now, as I write this, I know she is correct. I am sick when I think what I considered. How could I even have thought of such an evil thing?

I suddenly felt my attention drift. There was something in the diary that meant more to me than a history report. In my mind, I saw Mr. Lee as a short man with a round face and black hair mixed with white. I imagined him in his last few days as his illness worsened, stooping over, his hands shaking. At the same time, I remembered my mom's hand reaching for her teacup.

"Excuse me, girls."

Mrs. Snyder was at the door again and I still had a handful of pages left to read. Carefully I gathered the pages of the diary and walked to the shelves with my back toward the door. When I got there I went through the motions of putting the manuscript away, but instead I unzipped my jacket and slid the whole thing inside. Isabel watched me, her mouth dropping open in horror. She mouthed something to me, but I just walked along the table toward the door.

"So, are you girls all set?" Mrs. Snyder asked.

"Oh, yes. Thanks. We really have what we need now," I said, holding my arms across my chest to keep the diary from shifting. "But I'd like to come back again. I mean 'we' would. Could we?"

Mrs. Snyder smiled. "Of course. You'll have to."

She lead us to the door and held it open for us. "Give me a call when you're ready," she said.

I nodded and blinked as I stepped out into the afternoon sun. It was like I'd just stepped out of a matinee at the theater; it was so bright and warm outside.

Isabel followed me down the steps and grabbed my arm as I stepped onto the sidewalk.

"How could you have taken that diary?"

"I didn't steal it or anything. I mean not really. I just borrowed it."

"Sure, Margie, you *borrowed* it, the same way you borrow from a library — you just stuff it inside your shirt when nobody's looking."

"You don't understand, Isabel …"

"No, Margie, I don't. And I don't want to have to bring you your homework in jail, either."

"But I didn't *steal* it. I didn't even mean to take it. I meant to put it back on the shelf and I thought I was putting it back. My hand was tucking the diary into my jacket while my mind was saying to put it back on the shelf."

"Margie, that doesn't make any sense!"

"It doesn't make any sense to me, either," I blurted. "It was like I needed the diary, Isabel. It has something to do with my mother."

"Margie ..." Isabel started. I waited for her to continue, but she didn't. I guess she didn't know what else to say.

Finally, she asked, "what did Mrs. Snyder mean about us having to come back."

"I suppose she meant I would have to come back to return the manuscript." I thought about that moment when something inside me said to 'take it.' Somehow, I felt I had a right to borrow it.

"She knows you took the diary?" Isabel asked.

I nodded. "It sure looked like it." I hesitated. "But if she did know, why didn't she stop me?"

< 5 >

The Experiment

Mom and Dad were home when I got back from Mrs. Snyder's. I was happy to see them, but Mom seemed so fragile. I didn't know if she really looked different or if I was just seeing her differently.

She was tired. She said it was from the tests and the drive. I didn't question her about it, but later, after she went up to take a nap, I found Dad in the living room. I was determined to find out what he knew.

"Dad," I said.

He had been shuffling through a magazine, turning pages without looking at them. He looked up when I came in, closed the magazine and set it on the coffee table.

"I trust the Molinas took good care of you."

I nodded.

He was silent for a minute, then he started talking slowly, as if he wasn't sure how to form the words.

"You're worried about mom."

I swallowed and nodded.

"I wish there was more I could tell you. It seems like they've been looking everywhere, but they haven't looked in the right place yet."

"How serious is it?" I asked.

I was looking at him, trying to catch his eyes, but he wasn't making eye contact. "Well," he said, "I guess I wouldn't get worried about it yet."

"Is it getting worse?" I asked. "Are her symptoms getting worse?"

He didn't respond right away, but then he nodded his head slowly.

I felt tears well up in my eyes and then he was beside me, putting his arm around my shoulder and pulling me up against him.

"She's going to die, isn't she?" I whispered into his shoulder.

I felt his arm stiffen. He pulled away to look at me, but I didn't look up.

"Margie, of course not! She's got the best doctor in the State and the Center has a team of specialists going over the tests. I know they'll find out what's wrong with her. It's just a matter of time."

"Time," I said, softly, wondering how much more damage was being done as we sat in the shadowy living room, wondering how much longer Mom would live if they didn't find out something soon. Time hadn't helped Mr. Lee. He was dead. I thought about the diary and I remembered feeling that Mr. Lee's diary entries were connected to Mom's shaking hands.

"Dad," I said, suddenly, "I was working on a report and I read about this Chinese man. He lived in California back in the 1890s and he ..."

He patted me on the hand. "Margie ..."

"Dad, there's something about him that ..."

"I'm sorry, sweetheart, I'm a little distracted. I guess I'm not much of a listener these days. When all of this is over I promise I'll read your report."

"But, Dad ..."

Just then we heard Mom's voice from upstairs. I got

up, but Dad motioned me to stay while he went up, leaving me very confused and frightened.

~~~ ~~~ ~~~

Before bed, I went in to see Mom. She was sitting up, leaning against several pillows and staring toward the window. It was already after eight, so it was getting dark outside. The window was just a light gray rectangle in the darkness.

"Mom," I said, "what are you thinking about?"

"You, Margie," she said.

"What about me?"

"I'm thinking what a great kid you are. You are so strong and so smart, so pretty."

"Me? I'm not strong or pretty or smart."

She shook her head. "It's okay to be modest, Margie, but you also need to know the truth. You are really a wonderful person and I want to hear you say it."

"Mom," I said, embarrassed.

"Say it, Margie. If you say it, I'll know you accept it." She paused. "I want to hear you say 'I am a wonderful person.'"

I hesitated, knowing she was going to make me do it. It was awful. After a couple more seconds I said it, "I am a wonderful person."

"Believe in yourself, Margie. No matter what happens, you are wonderful and you have a lot to offer."

"Yes, Mom," I said, still embarrassed, but then I heard again what she said, 'no matter what happens.' What did she mean? I started walking to the door, my head spinning.

"Margie," Mom said when I reached the door, "sleep well and sleep tight."

It should have been comforting to hear the old phrase, but it wasn't working anymore.

"Good night, Mom," I said softly.

Sunday was supposed to be a family day, but Mom spent most of it in bed. She did come down for breakfast, but right after eating, she went back upstairs for a nap. As she struggled up the steps, I saw how thin and pale she looked, almost transparent. Dad went with her, joking about something or other, but holding her arm tightly all the way up.

I worked for about an hour on my Hebrew, chanting along with a tape of my Torah portion the Cantor had recorded. As I chanted it, I tried to follow along with the text, committing it to memory. The hardest part were the cantillations, the little marks that explain how the melody of the chanting goes. It was a struggle to get it right and to keep focused. The image of my mom and Dad on the stairs kept interfering.

When it was clear Mom would spend most of the day sleeping and Dad wasn't much in the mood to talk, I decided to go visit Isabel. Once again, I ended up spending the night there. It was a relief. Being in the house with Mom sick was so hard.

~~~ ~~~ ~~~

I finished reading the diary while Isabel washed the dinner dishes. There weren't many more entries. Mr. Lee's son wrote some about taking care of things after the funeral and about beginning to take over his father's work. There was also an envelope tucked into the last pages. It was empty, but very old and yellowed. It was addressed to Lee Yang in Fremont. I looked at the stamp and wondered if it was valuable. After all, it had been canceled a hundred years ago.

When Isabel finished the dishes I took over and dried. She started telling me more about Mr. Briones, the German stamp collector she was going to write about, while

I put the dishes away. I wasn't really listening at first. I was thinking about Mr. Lee, seeing his story kind of like a big jigsaw puzzle with a few pieces missing. It wasn't until Isabel started talking about Mr. Briones's strange time travel theory that I really started listening.

Helmut Briones was an eye doctor, whose German immigrant family moved to Cleveland in the middle 1860s just before he was born. Sometime in the late 1880s, he moved to Sacramento where he set up his office. His life seemed bleak as Isabel described it. He wasn't married and he didn't talk about friends. Maybe he didn't have many. He had only a few clients, but they gave him a small income, which allowed him to do what he really liked — collecting stamps.

Isabel told me how he wrote about his stamps, describing them like they were friends, talking about their flaws and how special that made them. Then Isabel told me about his strange belief that he could travel to the time and place where a stamp was canceled.

"Travel in time?" I asked.

"Yup, that's what he kept writing about."

"You mean like in *Back to the Future*?"

Isabel shook her head. "I don't know. He probably never saw *Back to the Future*."

I suddenly found myself thinking about my mom and Mr. Lee. Of course it was impossible to travel in time — wasn't it?

≈≈ ≈≈ ≈≈

I put the last pan in the cupboard and we went upstairs to Isabel's room. Her room had two beds on opposite walls. At the foot of Isabel's bed was a desk and across from it, at the foot of the other bed, was a dresser. There were the cross and the pictures of Jesus. It was weird for me when I slept overnight having Jesus looking down at me, especially when I was practicing for my Bat Mitzvah.

Once, when I thought Isabel was asleep, I looked up at the picture of Jesus, lit up by a street lamp outside and said, "you seem like such a nice Jewish boy!"

Isabel didn't say anything then. She didn't even move, but the next day at school it was all she could talk about. She thought it was the funniest thing she'd ever heard. It echoed through the school most of the morning. I tried to keep a low profile that day until the laughter died down.

<center>~~~ ~~~ ~~~</center>

Mrs. Molina agreed to let us stay up a little later than usual to work on our reports that night. We were brainstorming about how we could connect Mr. Lee's story and Mr. Briones's story so the reports could tie together. Isabel was pacing and talking in rhythm.

"How about this? We have Mr. Briones travel back in time to visit Mr. Lee. They can meet on the road or something and …"

"No," I said. "They lived at the same time. It doesn't make sense."

"Well," Isabel said, quickly. "He doesn't have to travel far back in time. Maybe he's just doing an experiment and somehow gets hold of a stamp from Mr. Lee."

I started laughing.

"What's so funny?" Isabel asked.

"I have a stamp from Mr. Lee — actually it's on a letter to Mr. Lee."

"You're kidding."

"No," I said, "I have it right here." I reached for the manuscript lying on the desk. I shuffled through the pages and pulled out the envelope. "Here's the stamp."

"Let me see that," Isabel said, reaching for it.

I handed it to her and sat back. "Pretty neat, huh, a real stamp from 1894! A hundred years ago that letter got delivered to Mr. Lee. Actually, I don't know which

Mr. Lee. Was it the father or the son?"

"Well, you could go back yourself and find out."

"Hey, now that would make a great paper. Boylan would definitely go for that."

"Yeah, he'd probably flunk you," Isabel said.

"No he wouldn't. He said he wanted me to keep the historical stuff alive and this is definitely lively. See, I'll set it up just like your guy said and go through all the motions to go back in time. Then I'll make up the rest based on the diary."

"That's what you're going to write for your report?"

"Exactly. Now how did this Briones guy say he did it?"

Isabel picked up her notebook and started scanning it. "It was some kind of silly pretend scientific mumbo-jumbo. Let's see, here it is. I'll read it to you:

"When I find the correct stamp, I must arrange things most carefully. I must lie down with tallow candles on either side of my head, focusing the light energy. I will do it on the night of a full moon at midnight when night and day become each other and time itself is confounded."

"What does he mean by 'confounded'?"

"I don't know, it's probably just some aphorism."

Isabel gave me a sly, sideways look. "It means a 'saying,'" she said, then continued reading. I would have called it an Isabelism.

"As the time approaches I will position myself directly in the light of the moon and place the stamp upside down on my forehead in the moonlight. Upside down will send me back. The moon is a witness to all earthly time and will conspire with the light of the candles to send me flying across the ethers of time."

"Across the ethers of time," I repeated, laughing. "Very poetic even if he didn't know diddle about science. I prefer Mr. Lee's approach. He was hoping to do an autopsy on his father to find out what killed him."

"He was? That's gruesome — and his own father."

"His sister wouldn't let him though. It was some kind of Chinese cultural taboo."

"Well, I should think so," Isabel blurted. "I'm sure my culture wouldn't allow a child to cut up his own father for research."

"Yeah, you're right, but what if he could find out what had caused him to die? What if it led to something like penicillin that saved millions of people? Wouldn't that be worth breaking a taboo?" I didn't mention that he might find out something that could help my mother.

"I don't know, Margie. That kind of question makes my skin crawl."

I nodded and picked up the envelope from Isabel's bed. The stamp was peeling up so I pulled on the corner and it came off in my hand.

"So let's do it. Isn't it a full moon tonight?"

Isabel looked at her calendar. "Now isn't that a coincidence?"

"There are no coincidences," I said in my Twilight Zone voice.

I stood up. "Help me move the bed."

Isabel grabbed one side and I grabbed the other. We kind of lifted it and slid it until the head was right against the sill.

"Okay," I said, "now you get two tallow candles and matches while I get in the mood for a rendezvous with the past so I can fly across the ethers of time."

I arranged the pillow to support my head and lay down on the bed. It was strange having my head in the moonlight. It felt like I was under some kind of cold ray. In a minute, Isabel returned, giggling, with the candles, the same kind of candles I'd used on Shabbat. Neither of us thought they were tallow, but they were all she had. She set them on the windowsill in their matching ceramic holders, then carefully lit them.

"All right," I said, tapping my forehead, "this is where the passport goes."

Isabel picked up the stamp and stared at it. "This is really silly, isn't it?"

I winked at her. "Of course it is, bubbala. We're a couple of silly girls."

"Are we forgetting anything?" she asked.

"I don't know. I don't think so."

I was ready, but she hadn't put the stamp on my forehead yet. "What's the matter, Isabel?" I was getting anxious; it was almost midnight.

"I don't know, I have this uneasy feeling we're forgetting something really important."

I lay there for a moment and closed my eyes. Were we forgetting something? After a second I felt Isabel touch my forehead and then the tickle of the stamp.

"I know what we forgot," Isabel said suddenly.

"What?"

"We forgot about ..."

I waited with my eyes closed, the tickle of the stamp still on my forehead in the cool light of the moon. I felt her weight shift on the bed and heard her rummaging around in her desk.

"About what, Isabel?"

There was no answer and I opened my eyes.

"Isabel, why did you turn out the light?" I gasped, "and what happened to the moon?"

< 6 >

A WHOLE NEW LANDSCAPE

I couldn't see anything. The room was as dark as a cave. I wasn't even sure my eyes were open until they began to adjust to the dribble of light coming from the other end of the room. The shape of a window slowly emerged and for a minute, all I could see was the square of faint light. This wasn't Isabel's room, for sure. I sat up and turned around, but everything was invisible except for that window. Slowly, the shapes of tall trees began to emerge from the background outside. I got up and walked carefully to the window, feeling for anything in the way. I brushed against a table before I made it to the sill and touched the glass. It was even colder than the air in the room.

There was no way this was real. It had to be a dream, but it wasn't like any dream I'd ever had before. For one thing, I'd never been cold in a dream. I was so disoriented that for a minute I didn't even know where I should have been. Then I remembered Isabel, the moon, and the stamp.

I touched my forehead, but, of course, the stamp was gone. It must have fallen off when I walked to the window. I made my way back to the bed. My eyes were beginning to work and I could see enough in the room to find my way around. I saw the door and walked to it but I couldn't find a light switch anywhere.

Somewhere, not too far off, I heard the sound of a clock ticking and the breathing of someone deep in sleep. A chill crept slowly up my spine to the base of my skull where it stuck like an ice cube. Where was I?

I walked back to the door and turned the knob gently, opening the door slowly so it wouldn't make any noise. The hallway was as dark as the room, but I could see a central stairwell with rooms around it. Above me was a skylight with only the slightest evidence that there was a sky out there that must have some light — streetlights, the moon, stars. I put my hand on the rail and followed it around until I got to the head of the stairs. There was a little more light downstairs from the windows around the entryway and coming from the open rooms on either side.

I needed to get out of the house to look around, to figure out where I was. The front door was unlocked and swung open quietly, but the air outside was cold. I eased the door closed and went down the stairs to the yard. The sky was overcast, and a thick layer of fog lay on the ground. A ghost of the full moon showed through a thin spot in the clouds. The little bit of light filtering down seemed eerie, and there wasn't even a breath of wind.

I walked across the slippery, wet grass. I was glad I had my sweater. It helped a little, although it was mostly for looks, not warmth. I hugged myself and shivered.

I purposely walked some distance from the house before I turned around, both to get a better idea of the surroundings and so I could see the whole house in one glance. Stopping just short of a small stand of trees, I turned.

It was a beautiful house, white and large, like a rich person's house. There were no houses around and no lights anywhere. No porch light, no streetlights, no headlights, no lights period. Then I remembered the wall next to the door in the room. No lights, no switches. There was no electricity!

Everything stood absolutely still around me. I looked at the house. Then I figured it out.

This was the Patterson House, the restored, turn-of-the-century farm at Ardenwood in Fremont, California. My stupid brain had come up with the only historical place I'd ever seen firsthand. So my experiment had come to this — I'd dreamed up the Patterson House. Big deal!

I shivered and clutched my arms more tightly. I turned once around in a circle and headed back to my dream house. I found my way to the kitchen and got as close as I could to the old wood stove which was still warm.

After a few minutes the chill was gone and I headed up the stairs in what I now recognized was the older part of the Patterson house. When I reached the top I peeked into a small room. Two boys had joined my dream. They lay in beds on opposite sides of the room, snoring away. I stepped in and looked around. It was my dream, after all, and I had a right to explore it.

One of the boys, the closest one, rolled over in his sleep. One eye popped open and he stared at me with a one-eyed look of surprise. Then his eye closed and his snoring started again. I went back into the hall and returned to the room where I had awakened.

I shivered going back inside. I thought about leaving the door open so some heat could come in, but that felt strange. Even in a dream, I wanted a little privacy.

I took off my shoes and climbed back into bed with my clothes on. The covers were heavy and warm and I quickly fell asleep, not even thinking about the fact that I had never gone to sleep in a dream before.

〰〰〰

I awoke from my dream of Ardenwood feeling cozy and

rested. I could sense Isabel lying opposite me on the other bed, but I kept my eyes closed.

For a little while I'd allowed myself to believe I could really go back in time, that there was something there for me — and that I could help, but the dream was over. I lay there in the soft, flannel sheets feeling cozy but disappointed.

Flannel? Isabel's sheets weren't flannel. My eyes shot open and I sat up. I looked over to Isabel's bed, but there was no bed. There was only a chair — and sitting in the chair was the boy who'd looked at me, one-eyed, the night before.

I stared at him. I blinked. I shook my head. He was still there.

"Who are you?" I asked.

He stared at me without saying a word.

"Where am I?" I hesitated. When he didn't answer I said, "This is the Patterson House, isn't it?

His blank expression changed to one of confusion. Finally, he opened his mouth.

"What are you doing here?" he asked.

"I don't know. I guess I'm dreaming," I said. "How about you?"

He paused, looking at me strangely. "Well I guess I'm not dreaming. This is where I live." He shook his head. "So how could you be dreaming?"

"I don't know. But a dream is a dream, you know."

"Well," he said hesitantly. "No, I don't really know at all."

I thought about that for a while, but I figured that characters in dreams were not particularly reliable so I didn't worry too much about it.

"What year is it anyway?" I asked.

"It's 1894, of course."

1894! Just like the stamp — and I'd figured out something else. This was Henry Patterson. I knew about him from the times I'd visited Ardenwood Farms, once with my class on a field trip and once with Isabel and her mother. He was the younger of two brothers in the Patterson family, and here he was talking to me. Some dream!

Henry took a long breath and asked me where I was from.

"Pluto," I said quickly, my teasing reflex kicking in.

"Where's that?" he asked.

I pointed toward the window. "Out there!" I said dramatically, "up in the sky. Pluto is a planet. Did you miss school the day they talked about astronomy?"

His expression turned suddenly into a big grin.

"I just knew it," he said. "I knew you were from another planet. I was thinking more of Venus. Yesiree! This is really great!"

I shook my head slowly.

"I'm from Berkeley," I said flatly. "You know Berkeley? The Cal Bears? Telegraph Avenue? People's Park?"

He nodded as he watched me, looking very disappointed. "I've heard of Berkeley. I think I have. But why did you say Pluto?"

I shrugged. "I was only kidding."

He looked so disappointed that I thought I should cheer him up by telling him the truth.

"But I am from the future — 1994," I said dramatically.

"The future?" he asked. He was starting to smile again, a little suspiciously this time, but I could tell he was pleased.

Henry was alarmed when I pulled back the covers, but he realized quickly that I was dressed. That's when his alarm turned to surprise.

"You're wearing pants!" he said, almost shouting in surprise.

"Henry?" a voice came from down the hall.

Henry slapped his hand over his mouth. Then he took it off and whispered, "That's my brother, William."

"You'd better answer him," I whispered, "or he's going to come in to find out what's going on."

"But what should I say?"

"I don't know. Tell him breakfast will be ready soon."

Henry turned toward the closed door. "Breakfast will be ready soon."

"Oh," William's voice came through the door. "Okay, I'll be down in a minute."

Henry turned back to me with a pleased expression, obviously satisfied with our deception. I suddenly felt guilty that I was teaching this boy to lie, but that was silly. Surely he was already a pretty good liar.

His eyes went to my Levi's again.

"Girls don't wear pants," he said.

"Maybe not in your time," I answered.

That's when he started asking me questions. I had a great time telling him about computers, television, microwave popcorn, Carmen San Diego, roller blades, 18-speed bikes and light bulbs, although it was clear he wasn't following me. It really made me think about all the things around us we rely on but never think about. Indoor plumbing — when you think of it, it's a pretty big deal.

What surprised Henry most was that everybody had electric lights — and plumbing. I guess microwaves and Carmen San Diego were way beyond him and roller blades probably didn't make any sense at all if you hadn't spent much time in a city with sidewalks. I was sure he'd never seen a parking lot.

I could see his mouth working as he prepared to ask me a dozen more questions, but then a voice came from downstairs and I jerked in surprise.

"My mother," Henry said quickly. "I don't think she should know you're here." He paused, thinking. "I'll sneak some breakfast up to you in a little while, but you'll have to stay here until I can figure out a good time to get you out." He stopped halfway out the door and turned back. "I guess this is really something, isn't it?"

I felt like a prisoner in that room for the next few hours. I had to be careful not to make the floor creak so I didn't walk much and I surely couldn't get out of the house unseen with all of the activity going on downstairs.

Henry finally brought me some melon and then sneaked me out late in the morning. His idea was to take me over to a house nearby where Daniel, the Pattersons' farmhand, lived. The farmhand, Henry said, was a friend and would help us. I didn't know what this Daniel was supposed to help us with, but I went along with him. Fortunately, everyone at the Patterson house was busy with chores so getting out turned out to be easy.

The chill of my early morning exploration was gone as we walked through the trees. We were heading west, to where the parking lot would be in another 70 or 80 years. We walked for a couple minutes in and out of trees until I saw something moving up ahead; it was a big brown mare.

Henry had brought her out of the barn and tied her to a tree in preparation for our escape. He was surprised when I walked right up to her and patted her side. I think he figured I would naturally be afraid of horses, being a girl and all. Then I got my surprise. The mare was decidedly pregnant.

"We can't ride her."

"Why not?"

I pointed to her.

"Look at her. She's pregnant."

Henry laughed. "She's not ready for birthing yet and we only have to go a couple miles."

"A couple miles and she'll go into labor!" I said, furiously. "Stupid boys. You don't know anything, do you?"

Henry was struck dumb. I don't think he'd ever run into anyone like me before. Maybe no girls ever came out here. I'd never thought of myself as being all that

assertive, but maybe that just came naturally with growing up in the 80s and 90s. I mean, of course, the 1980s
and 1990s. Henry walked over to the horse and leaned
against the saddle.

"Are you okay, girl?" he asked. He rubbed her neck.

I lowered my voice so it was less know-it-all.

"Maybe you should take the saddle off. The cinches
might be hurting her, pulling against her stomach like
that."

He didn't look at me, but he nodded. Immediately
he began undoing the saddle. He slid it off and set it
down near the tree.

I could see by the horse's breathing that she was relieved and I knew Henry could see it too.

I realized that, even though he was hopelessly dumb,
he really did care about the horse, and I thought about
all the dumb things I'd done because I'd gotten caught
up in an idea that was too good to let go.

Finally, he turned to me. "Do you think we could ride
her without the saddle? Would that hurt her?"

I knew it would be foolish, that it was a tremendous
risk, but I also could see how disappointed Henry was. I
really wanted to do what was best for everyone. I
shrugged.

"I guess if we ride her very carefully and slowly, she
might be okay."

His face brightened and he almost smiled at me. It
wasn't the initial, self-satisfied smile I'd seen in the
Pattersons' guestroom. This one was a little more careful. I think he was afraid of me.

He turned back to the horse. "Nelly, is it okay if we
ride? This is very important."

Nelly neighed which Henry took to mean that she
agreed. He turned to me.

"Can you ride without a saddle?" he asked. He took
my scowl as a 'yes,' then climbed up on her back. I took
his hand and got up behind him. Immediately I knew it

was a mistake. I was sure I was right about her and I could feel her labored breathing. My mom says that I have a real knack for animals just like she does and my horse sense said this was too much for her. I reluctantly held onto Henry's jacket for balance and we were on our way.

I was sort of expecting a dirt road, but there was no road at all. At one point we even had to cross a stream. I felt like I was in a Bonanza rerun.

I normally would have enjoyed the ride even sitting behind someone else, but I was constantly tense, stupidly trying to keep my weight off Nelly's back — as if there was anywhere else for it to go.

After a while I noticed Nelly was breathing even harder and I suggested in my least assertive voice that we stop.

Henry insisted we continue. "We're nearly there," he said with assurance. Just then we saw a thin man of medium height racing toward us. It was Daniel.

"Get off the horse! Get off."

Immediately Henry reined in the horse. I got down first; then Henry got down.

"Oh, my poor Nelly," Daniel said. He was a young Chinese man who obviously knew all about Nelly's condition. Something in my brain tried to surface, but he was so frantic and I suddenly felt so guilty about riding Nelly that I couldn't think of it. He handed me the reins and led us along the riverside path. When we reached his house a few minutes later, he ran inside to grab a horse blanket that he threw over Nelly's back.

"Now, my friend Henry," he said, "this was a very bad thing. I trust your parents do not allow this. They would not have let you take Nelly out so close as she is to foaling." He put his head against the horse's side and listened intently for a minute. "I hope we have not started things too early. Early foals are very difficult to keep and sometimes the mothers, too, have trouble."

Henry hung his head and he wouldn't look at either of us. He was ashamed of himself for putting Nelly at risk and obviously embarrassed that I was right.

"Do not be too angry with yourself, Henry. If damage was done, it is too late to fix, and you will not do foolishness like that again."

Henry nodded slightly, then he walked over to Nelly and stood looking at her.

The farmhand turned to me.

"Ah, you are the girl from the future," he said. I saw his eyes as he looked at my jeans, but he didn't really react.

"How did you know?" I asked.

He gave me a mysterious smile. "Henry came here this morning and said he would bring you later. His description was not fully right, but not so far off, either. You are very pretty girl. Henry did say that."

I looked over at Henry who pretended to be interested in the tree that stretched its branches over the cabin. He was blushing.

"Your name is?" the man asked.

"Margie. Margie Belzer."

"They call me Daniel," he said, smiling.

After letting Nelly rest for a while, Henry started back, leading her by the reins. Henry promised he would stop several times along the way to let Nelly rest. I wondered what he would do at the stream. Would he take off his shoes and walk across? Would he climb on Nelly to keep his feet dry crossing the stream? I was almost confident that he wouldn't.

∼∼∼ ∼∼∼ ∼∼∼

Daniel motioned me into the house and held out a chair. He poured some green tea and offered me some biscuits. Then he sat across from me at the small table in the small, cramped kitchen, just a corner of the house with a sink, and a shelf for a few pans and dishes. It seemed a harsh place to live. There was no rug or carpet and no couches or pictures on the wall. There were a couple of simple, worn curtains and a bedspread, but everything else was wood.

Daniel looked at me as if he were reading a book. It only took a minute for me to become uncomfortable with the silence, but for some reason I knew enough not to start chattering to fill it.

After some time, he nodded as if he was satisfied.

"So, girl from the future, it is good to see things are not changed so much. Although I do see that shoes are greatly changed."

I stuck out my foot and Daniel looked at my high-top Reeboks.

"These are very complicated shoes. Not sewn like most."

"No, I guess not," I said. "I supposed they must be glued or something in some huge factory where they make a thousand or so every minute."

"No!" Daniel said, shocked.

I smiled and shrugged my shoulders.

"They cost almost $70."

"Seventy dollars?"

I nodded and Daniel whistled.

"I have never seen $70 shoes before. Except in bank, I think I have not seen $70 in one place." Then he tapped his teeth gently. "I have also never seen so much metal in a mouth either. What is this?"

I felt myself blush. I don't like wearing braces.

"Braces," I said quietly.

"Mouth jewelry?" Daniel asked innocently.

"No, they straighten teeth that grow in crooked."

I could see his tongue moving around inside his mouth as he was thinking.

"Maybe I should have them," he said, smiling widely so I could see how crooked his own teeth were. They were far worse than any I'd ever seen.

Daniel picked up the teapot and poured more tea in both cups. Then he looked at me seriously.

"I must tell you, Margie, I do not like being untruthful. Yet I told young Henry I would help him. So I become part of a secret against his parents. I believe that it must be a good cause and yet even Henry does not guess what it is. I hope you may explain it to me."

I hesitated, wondering how to explain the complex story and suddenly heard a voice calling from outside. I looked through the rough curtains covering the window next to me. Henry Patterson's older brother was riding in on another horse and calling for Daniel.

Daniel stood up quickly. "Stay here. William will not come in and I will not need to explain." Then he walked out and met William, who started talking as soon as the door opened.

"Daniel, you have to come at once. Henry has gone and ridden Nelly and now she's getting ready to deliver. We need your help."

"You go back, William. Tell your father I will get my things and follow you. Now go!"

I watched as William galloped up the path. Immediately, Daniel came back into the cabin and grabbed a cloth bag. He glanced in it quickly and closed it.

"I will come back as soon as I can. Please to make yourself at home."

I looked at him with sudden curiosity. "Why do they need your help?"

Daniel turned toward the door. "I care for the animals," he said, hurrying out of sight toward the back of the house. Soon he reappeared on a beautiful brown horse and paused by the front door.

"I will see you soon, Margie from the future."

"Daniel," I called urgently, "what is your real name?"

"Lee," he said as he rode off, "Lee Yang."

< 7 >

CONNECTIONS

My hands were suddenly cold and a shiver traveled down my spine, very slowly, like it wasn't sure where it was going. The pieces had all fallen into place, but it was way too neat. Here I was in the house of Lee Yang, the son of Lee Chau Wing. I hadn't figured it out sooner because the Pattersons called him Daniel. How long had it been since his father died? I tried to remember the date of the last diary entry. Was it August or September?

I looked around for a calendar, but I couldn't find one. As my eyes traveled the room, I began to see that the lack of things and gadgets was kind of soothing. There was something almost poetic about it. Daniel, or his father maybe, had created a home without all the extras. Of course, there wasn't a CD player or lamps, or a microwave, but there were other things missing I couldn't even name, and it came to me that if I couldn't think of them, maybe they weren't necessities at all.

There was one thing in the room that wasn't so organized. Along the wall next to the bed was an old desk. Even then, one hundred years ago, the desk was obviously old. It was out of place in this careful house with simple, straight lines and rough-sawed boards. The desk was not large, but it had curving surfaces and a carved drawer front.

I walked over, sat down and immediately felt at ease. At the back of the desk was a collection of books, some in English, but many in Chinese — anyway, it looked Chinese. On the desktop were a couple fountain pens and a bottle of ink. On the right side was a large and very old-looking book in Chinese, open to just about the middle, with its columns of complicated small figures. On the left side was a microscope with a small wooden box which looked like a dissection kit. Near that was an oil lamp on a stack of loose pages. The pages were handwritten in English. I paused for a second, staring at the top page. Then my breathing stopped.

Carefully, I lifted the oil lamp off the paper and set it aside. The writing was more than familiar. It was a diary page and I knew what it said by heart:

September 3: *Today we said good-bye to father.*

Here was the same diary in the same handwriting — only the paper was almost white and smooth. Lee Yang had not written another page, but why? Then my eyes found a small calendar with the days carefully crossed off. The last day crossed off was September 7. Four days had passed since his father died and Lee Yang hadn't written any more in the diary.

My head was spinning. All these coincidences had made me think it was all a dream. Then just one more coincidence and suddenly I was convinced this wasn't a dream at all. I had actually gone back in time and maybe I could find out something that would help my mother. I was wondering if Daniel had written any more pages about his father's death, and at the same time I was thinking that if he had I would already know it — wouldn't I? But what was to stop him from writing some more now, even as I watched, and what would that mean? Could some pages that he hadn't even written yet have disappeared before I found them at Mrs. Snyder's house?

I closed my eyes and leaned my head on my hands. After a few minutes, I couldn't stand thinking about it anymore. I got up and went out. Seeing the water pump, I realized how thirsty I was. I stopped to get a drink, pumping on the iron handle without success. Then I saw a can of water on a box next to the pump and the phrase "priming the pump" popped into my mind. I needed to have water in the pump for the pump to work. I grabbed the can and carefully poured the water in where the metal bar went up and down. When it had disappeared into the holes, I tried again, pumping just a few times before the water gushed into and all over the can I was holding. I shook the spilled water off my hand and took a drink. It was cold and it cleared my mind.

I made sure the can was filled again. Then I headed up a small hill west of Daniel's house. I felt warmer as the path climbed out of the shade of the trees into the sunlight.

At the top of the hill, I looked out to the west. There was the Bay just about a half-mile away. I knew it was the San Francisco Bay even though it looked so different. It was much bigger and closer. I remember reading about how the Bay has been filled in during the last hundred years. I was also surprised how many trees were between the water and me.

I looked for the San Mateo Bridge which, of course, hadn't been built yet. Somewhere on the other side of the Bay was Palo Alto. In a hundred years, my mother would be there in a fancy hospital surrounded by all of the newest medical equipment.

A minute later I saw movement through the trees down by Daniel's cabin. I watched and soon a horse appeared. I could see it was Daniel. I turned and headed back down the hill.

Daniel was in the kitchen when I got back to his cabin. He was washing some vegetables in a bowl.

"Hello, Margie. Nelly foaled today. I do not know yet what will happen. The foal came too early. Nelly was very weak when I left, lost much blood. But I did all I could do for her."

"I tried to talk Henry out of riding her ..." I stopped, feeling ashamed for trying to cover up the part I played. "In the end, I just gave in."

Daniel nodded, but didn't say anything. He just looked at me and it made me feel foolishly young.

I waited quietly as he went back to washing. I knew what I wanted to ask, but somehow I couldn't break the silence.

He turned to me. "You will have dinner with me?" he asked.

"Daniel?"

"Yes, Margie."

"What happened to your father?"

"He died. A very good man, but he died."

"But do you know what he died of?" I crossed my fingers and my eyes, hoping for the right answer.

Daniel slowly shook his head.

"Then you didn't do the autopsy?"

Daniel looked startled. "How do you know about that?"

"From your diary. I mean your father's diary."

"You read the diary while I was gone? Margie, I did not think I needed to ask you not to look at private things."

"I didn't read the diary."

"Then how?"

"I mean I did read it, but not while you were gone. I saw it on your desk, but I read it before I came back to this time. It's the reason I came back."

"Before you came back ...? I do not understand."

"Your father's diary is in a collection of historical society books."

"In your time?"

I nodded.

He shook his head very slowly, digesting what I'd said. "It is very strange to think my father is part of history, most strange! In a way, father lives on in this diary."

"Yes, and your father and you wrote about something that caused me to come back in time."

"But you must explain …"

I looked at Daniel. His stare was so intense, almost hypnotic. Suddenly my real life started coming back to me in flashes. My house, my school, Isabel, and my mother — mostly my mother, in the restaurant, that awful Monday morning in the kitchen and the days that followed.

"Your father and my mother," I started, and my eyes felt suddenly hot.

⁓⁓ ⁓⁓ ⁓⁓

It took a while to tell it all. It was hard because it brought all of it back, including all my fears, but I struggled through to the end. When I finished, Daniel was staring at me. Then he nodded.

Daniel and I sat at his small table eating rice and vegetables. He was thinking, looking over my shoulder through the open window.

"And so," he began, "you hoped I would find something to help your mother."

I nodded. "But you didn't do the autopsy …?"

"No, unburying the dead is very bad, and what I planned to do …"

He looked at me closely. "I hoped to learn how my father died. It is such a waste to die and not even learn anything from it, but Chinese culture is very strong. There is a line connecting us to China even here. Respect for ancestors is the most important thing."

"And my mother?" I asked suddenly, my tone sharp. "She's not important?"

Daniel looked at me for a long time.

"You must understand ..."

"I don't understand. I won't understand."

Daniel nodded.

Tears began streaming down my cheeks, but I kept my eyes locked on his.

"I am sorry, Margie. So very sorry."

〰 〰 〰

William Patterson came to Mr. Lee's cabin a little while later. Fortunately, I was out in the woods trying to walk off my frustration. It was fortunate because William was looking for me. I returned after William had already gone, and found Daniel carefully gathering together clothes and food. There were sheets hanging from the ceiling, separating one corner of the cabin from the rest. I was about to ask him what was happening when he started talking.

"Henry has done a terrible thing."

I looked at him. "What do you mean?"

"Nelly died. The foal is still struggling to keep alive. She will need to be fed by bottle. It will not be easy."

I closed my eyes. I'd agreed that it was okay to ride Nelly and now she was dead. Just this morning she'd stood in the shade of the trees, a beautiful mare carrying her baby in her womb. Then I'd gone along with Henry's foolish idea, just to keep from hurting his feelings. "Henry didn't mean to," I said, "it was an awful mistake."

"It was your mistake, too, Margie, but that is not what I mean."

"What then?"

"Henry has told a horrible lie that may be more dangerous than we can know."

He hesitated, shaking his head.

"His father was very angry about Nelly. When he started talking about using a horsewhip, Henry made up stories. He said that a strange girl took horse, that he went after her to get it back."

"He what?"

"He lied to place blame on you so he would not be horsewhipped."

I was shocked.

"But that's not true. I tried to talk him out of riding Nelly. I knew that it was a risk. But I didn't know …"

"You and Henry made a mistake and now Henry has made a most serious lie. His father will come tomorrow morning to find out the truth."

"And will you tell him?"

"No," he said, pointing to the things on the table, "we will not be here."

I shook my head, not understanding. "Then they'll believe him."

Daniel sat down at the table. "No, they will wonder why I am gone, but they will not believe Henry. Without you, his story is not believable."

Daniel's voice dropped almost to a whisper.

"They must not find you. They must not know that you have come to us."

"But why?"

"Because it is not right. There is something dangerous about your visit to us across time. Do you understand?"

I shook my head; I couldn't think that fast.

"Only Henry and I know you are here so far. That is probably not much impact because Henry is only a boy and I am only a Chinaman. But if the Pattersons learn that you, a girl from the future, are really here, it might change things for you, for your time. I think this is very dangerous and I worry for you."

Finally, it began to make sense. If I did something that changed what happened here and now, maybe it would change the things that led up to my time. I had read that in books before, but it had just seemed like part of the plot. Now, suddenly, it seemed frighteningly possible.

"What are we going to do?"

"I am taking you to Stockton. We will visit my sister for two or maybe three days and we will think of how we might get you back to your time. When I return and Mr. Patterson asks me about you, I will not understand. I will be confused and soon even Henry will remember you only like a dream."

"But what about your sister? If we go there, she will know I am here, too."

"Yes and her daughters as well, but they speak little English and you will be only a mystery to them. You will not make so big an impression, I hope."

I stood there stupidly until he pointed to an empty corner of the room.

"You will sleep there. I will make you a bed. You should get ready now because we must leave early. I have more things to gather, but I will also go to bed as soon as I have what we need."

‹ 8 ›

JOURNEY TO STOCKTON

I woke early to the twitter of birds, the neighing of a horse, and the sound of Daniel fixing breakfast. The sky was just beginning to lighten as I got dressed — in the same clothes I'd been wearing for the past two days. The jeans hadn't seen the inside of a washing machine in more than two weeks and I felt grungy for sure.

Daniel had eaten and left cut apples and steamed rice on the table for me. As I ate I heard him bringing the horse around and hitching it to his wagon.

I was practicing my Torah portion when Daniel came in. He heard the Hebrew words and saw my lips moving.

"Is this a language from the future, Margie?"

I laughed. "No. It's actually one of the oldest languages around."

"Older even than Chinese?" Daniel looked shocked.

I shook my head. "Well, I don't know. How old is Chinese?"

"Oh, it is very ancient."

"Hmmm … well maybe Chinese is older, but Hebrew goes way back to the time of the pyramids in Egypt. It is the traditional language of the Jewish people."

"You are Jewish?"

I smiled.

"I have never met a Jewish person before."

⁓⁓ ⁓⁓ ⁓⁓

The road to Stockton was just a pair of parallel, wagon-wheel ruts cutting through the hard, dry ground. I could tell that the ruts had been formed during the rainy season. The ground seemed to be nothing but bumps and holes, and the wagon tilted and tossed like a rowboat in a storm.

The sun grew hot as it rose. We stopped by a curving line of trees that made no sense until I saw that they followed a stream. Daniel handed me a porcelain bowl and we climbed onto a flat rock that stuck out into the stream. We sat there a few minutes, passing the bowl back and forth, drinking water straight from the stream. It was cool and clear. It tasted a little like bottled water only with flavor, good flavor. As I tipped the bowl back, a strange thought came to me: We were headed for Stockton, where Lee Chau Wing was buried.

⁓⁓ ⁓⁓ ⁓⁓

It was already getting dark before I realized we would not reach Stockton that night. Daniel kept riding and our eyes got used to the dark, but eventually he pulled the wagon into a grove of trees and took Gladys out of the harness. I helped him brush her and then led her to the stream for water. She grazed while I helped Daniel lay out the food he had brought: hard bread, homemade cheese and apples. It didn't seem like much of a dinner, but it tasted wonderful. Nothing was like I was used to. Even the apples were crisp, tart and sweet — the best I'd ever tasted.

While we were cleaning up and packing things back

in the wagon, I saw something wrapped up in a corner of the wagon. I stared at it, its shape still apparent through the blanket. It was his microscope. Why had he brought that with us now?

By the time we finished stowing things and preparing the bedding it was dark and cool. I was going to sleep in the wagon and Daniel would sleep on the ground. Fog slid in from the Bay. That made me feel at home in a way I hadn't felt since before Mom got sick. Daniel made a small campfire and we sat and talked.

"My sister's name is Lin Sun," he said. "I had an older brother, but he died of scarlet fever.

"Lin Sun has three daughters and no sons. This is not so good in China, but here it is maybe not so bad. Culture does not always travel so well. Lin Sun's youngest daughter is much trouble. Would be easier if Lin Sun had a husband, but he died on boat journey. They were almost to San Francisco and he became sick and died."

"What does her younger daughter do that makes her such a terror?"

"Oh, Mei Mei wants to be great painter, but only men are great painters. Lin Sun is very distressed and doesn't know what to do. Third daughter is very stubborn."

"Then she's probably a lot like me," I said.

"I was thinking that, also," Daniel said.

I looked at him to see what he meant. His eyes flashed and he smiled.

"I think that maybe all future girls are stubborn," he said, laughing.

"Some more than others," I said.

"I am most sure of that, Margie."

~~~ ~~~ ~~~

Daniel let the fire burn down and when I started getting cold, I climbed into the roll of blankets Daniel had helped me set up for my bed. He said goodnight and lay on the ground under the trees, with his horse nuzzling him.

After a minute I heard him speaking. I'm sure he was speaking to me, but his voice was so soft that it could almost have been the sound of him thinking.

"I think maybe time like a river. We are carried by current. Maybe we can climb out of current and get back in someplace else. Maybe we can."

~~~ ~~~ ~~~

I fell asleep imagining myself up on the bima, reading from the Torah — and for the first time, it wasn't a nightmare. I was nervous, but I felt ready to be up there in front of the congregation.

~~~ ~~~ ~~~

I awoke suddenly, confused about where I was and why. The sun was just creeping over the hills, an uneven line of bright light against a dark horizon with an orange blush on the bottom of the clouds. I could barely move in my twisted bedding. After a minute I stopped struggling and immediately things began to fall into place.

Daniel, who'd been hitching Gladys to the wagon, looked over and saw me.

"Ah, good! You are up," he said. "It is time we are moving so we make it to Stockton before dinner. I did not bring food for another dinner and breakfast, and I do not much like hunger. Also, Lin Sun is wonderful cook. Have you ever tasted Chinese food?"

I laughed. "Sure, I eat it all the time."

From the look on his face, it was clear he hadn't meant it as a serious question. Now he was closely examining me. "Your mother cooks Chinese food, then?" He stretched the question out as if the whole idea was too unlikely to say aloud.

"Well, no. My father makes fried rice sometimes, but

mostly we go to Chinese restaurants in Berkeley."

Daniel shook his head. "This is hard to believe. You mean there is more than one Chinese restaurant in Berkeley?"

"Oh, yes!" I said. "There are lots of Chinese restaurants in Berkeley, maybe 20 or 30!"

Daniel looked at me as if this were the strangest thing he'd ever heard.

"Berkeley must be a wonderful place. Everybody eats Chinese food all the time. What a wonderful future!"

I started to explain about Berkeley, about the hundreds of restaurants, about the gourmet ghetto, about people going out to eat because they didn't have time to prepare a meal, but then I stopped. What would it hurt if Daniel thought the future would be wonderful — full of Chinese restaurants! Besides, I didn't think he'd believe Berkeley has more than 100,000 people.

Absently, I pulled my hand from my pocket, finding the fortune the little girl had been so determined to give me on my birthday.

Daniel watched closely as I turned it over and took it when I held it out to him. He looked at it for a moment, then he found a pen and ink bottle in a bundle in the wagon.

"It is a very good fortune. I will write it for you so you can remember."

I watched him as he carefully wrote on the back of the slip of paper. He handed it back to me. In his very familiar script he'd written: "Believe in yourself."

~~~ ~~~ ~~~

We spent a long day in the wagon, bumping along toward Stockton. Daniel was quiet and I spent a lot of time thinking. Mostly I was thinking about my mother and Daniel's father. Maybe there was still a chance that we could find something. If only ...

Just as the sun was setting, our road became a street, not much more than another dirt path, but this one had houses along it. It wasn't like a city block today, just a house here and there with sheds and shops between. A couple of blocks ahead there were some bigger buildings, two stories of gray wood with signs painted on the sides. That must have been the main part of Stockton. We turned before we got there, away from the cluster of houses and buildings toward a separate cluster of small houses, close together, but very tidy. Daniel stopped at one, jumped down out of the wagon, and tied the horse to a tree. Gladys neighed with what seemed to be pleasure; she recognized the place.

A little girl came running out of the house, her round face smiling, her dark eyes peeking out from under straight, black bangs. She got almost to Daniel, a little whirlwind of a thing, before she saw me.

She stopped immediately, like a videotape on pause. All that energy suddenly gone or at least stuck in vibrating captivity. Her face, so bold and expectant, suddenly tilted forward and her eyes looked toward her feet. Her long ponytail slipped around over her shoulder.

Daniel took her hands and looked into her eyes.

He spoke rapidly in Chinese and she answered in quick, high tones — like music. Then Daniel turned her toward me.

He said something quickly in Chinese directed toward the girl, then said, "Margie, this is Lee Mei. We call her Mei Mei."

< 9 >

A CHINESE DINNER

I sat down while Daniel's sister and his three nieces brought out dishes and cups for the table with familiar designs I'd seen a hundred times at Cost Plus Imports. I could hear them talking in the kitchen, cooking a dinner for their unexpected guests. Soon the small house was full of delicious smells that made me realize how hungry I was.

I was just sitting there, content to wait, but suddenly it struck me that, although there was talking in the kitchen, none of Daniel's family spoke when they came into the small room where Daniel and I were sitting, not even in Chinese. I looked across at Daniel and he smiled, reading my mind.

"They have never had a guest not Chinese before. Usually the table buzzes with their talk, talk, talk." He carefully poured a cup of tea for me. "They will become warm to you."

Then, in an instant, everyone was seated. The table was full of wonderful food and I was nearly dizzy with hunger, but everyone just waited, looking toward the center of the table. I looked there, too, but there was nothing special to see.

"They are waiting for you to take some first and try it," Daniel explained. "Lin Sun made special dishes for us and the daughters helped her. They are excited and nervous in case you don't like it." He leaned toward me and lowered his voice to a whisper. "Please pretend that you do."

I smiled at him and scooped some cashew chicken from a large bowl onto the plate. I noticed a fork by my plate. I didn't even stop to wonder why they had a fork. It was bent and tarnished, but it would certainly work. I glanced at it, then picked up a pair of enameled chopsticks instead. As I arranged them in my hands and began to scoop up the rice one of the girls gasped.

I looked at Daniel and he smiled as I took a bite.

"You have made a most excellent impression, Margie. None in my family has ever seen a ghost eat with chopsticks before. But I suppose that every child in Berkeley must learn to eat with chopsticks to keep all those Berkeley restaurants busy."

I took another bite, nodding and smiling. The cashews were crispy and the chicken was tender and delicious. Then everyone else began to take food and eat.

"Please tell your sister this is the best cashew chicken I have eaten," I said between bites.

Daniel paused, thinking about that. Then he started talking. His sister kept looking at me with a puzzled expression as the conversation continued. The children ate as if they couldn't hear what was going on, but their eyes followed the conversation, sometimes looking at me.

As Daniel continued to talk with his sister, Mei Mei tugged on my sleeve. I turned to see what she wanted and saw that she was holding a plate with a single egg roll on it.

"For me?" I asked.

She nodded so I tilted the plate and let the egg roll slide onto my plate. Carefully I picked it up with my chopsticks and turned it to take a bite, but it slipped to my plate. Mei Mei laughed and I laughed.

"I make," she said.

I looked closely at her as she acted out filling the egg roll wrap, then carefully rolling and closing it. Her movements were so exact that I knew she had made many egg rolls. I lifted it, this time with my fingers and took a crunchy bite of it.

"It is delicious!" I said, trying to show all my pleasure in my face. The table had gotten quiet and Mei Mei flushed with pride. Slowly the table began to buzz again with their "talk, talk, talk" and I found myself on the outside. Daniel periodically would translate something for me, but finally he just seemed to get caught up in the pleasure of the food and his family. He relaxed into being a brother and uncle and left me to eat.

~~~ ~~~ ~~~

After dinner, Mei Mei took me to a room off the kitchen where there was a small table and a chair. She directed me to the chair and reached into a wooden crate on the floor, bringing out a pad of paper and a piece of charcoal. She handed them to me and stood as if posing.

"You want me to draw you?" I asked. She looked at me with a puzzled expression, then nodded eagerly, her hair shaking up and down.

"No I …" I wanted to explain that I was not artistic, but I knew that would be impossible to communicate so I just started drawing. She would find out soon enough.

It was funny when I finished and showed it to her. She tried to hide a giggle behind her hand. I don't think she wanted to hurt my feelings. Of course there was no way she could. I couldn't be trusted with a crayon and I knew it.

She smiled at me very diplomatically, then indicated she would draw me. I stood and assumed a pose I thought would show me in the best light. Unfortunately it was an awkward pose and Mei Mei took her time, looking, sketching, and looking. Soon I wanted to sit down, to stretch, to jump. It seemed forever before she let me know I was free again. It was like getting out of jail.

Then she showed me her drawing and my mouth dropped open. It was incredible! I'm not saying it was a Rembrandt or anything, but there was no question who she had drawn. She had even caught my discomfort with the pose — and it was not completely flattering. It was a great picture and I think she even improved on me here and there.

Holding tightly, she tore the page off the tablet. She was so exact in her movements that I realized this was a delicate operation. I guess perforations hadn't been invented yet.

"This is for me?" I asked.

She nodded.

"It's wonderful!"

I know she didn't understand my words, but I could tell by her face that she understood what I meant.

∿ ∿ ∿

Mei Mei was showing me some of her other drawings when Daniel came in. I had heard him talking with Lin Sun while Mei Mei was drawing. Their voices had been soft, but intense in the next room.

Daniel's face was pale as he looked at me and I thought again about my mother and Daniel's father. I'd been in the past for almost three days and I was losing a sense of reality about things. At times, my mom's illness seemed so unreal, but then it would come back at me. What was happening to her now? What might have happened already?

Daniel waited until I looked up at him. My eyes were warm and damp and I was sure he could see it.

"Margie?" Daniel said.

"Why am I here, Daniel?" I asked. "What does it mean?"

Daniel hesitated. "Lin Sun and I have talked."

I nodded, still feeling lost and not following him.

"We … I am going to visit my father a last time."

I continued to look at him, trying to understand.

"I will do what you asked."

I shook my head. "What?"

"I will do autopsy. My sister believes it the right thing."

I just stared at him.

"Margie, it is why you are here. Lin Sun agrees I must do this."

I swallowed. "But … what do you feel?"

"I must do this for you and for your mother. My feeling is not important."

∿ ∿ ∿

I could see in his eyes how he was struggling with the meaning of his decision. At the same time I saw that he was thinking of what it could mean, what it had to mean for my mother. I realized I was holding my breath and I slowly let it out.

"It is my father who I now will …" His voice trailed off. He shook his head. "This is a most horrible deed I now contemplate. How much easier to argue for this when sister opposed."

I gritted my teeth. "I'll help," I said, choking on the words, "of course."

"Oh, no, Margie. I do myself."

"But you'll need help."

"Margie, you do not even belong to us, to our time. You cannot risk."

"But you're doing it for my mom."

"That does not matter. I do alone. I will have help with digging, but then I will do the work alone."

I nodded, feeling relief at not having to help Daniel with such awful work — and guilty that I was the cause of it.

88

I didn't realize he would be going to his father's grave that night. It was already dark, and, as Daniel assembled his tools in the kitchen, including the microscope and several lanterns, it began to sink in what a fiendish thing this was — grave robbing, disturbing the dead. He had to do it secretly, in the black of night. I shuddered, feeling continuously cold as he moved through the house, boards creaking loudly under his feet. He seemed empty, like a robot without personality or feeling. Finally I heard the boards creak by the door and the squeaking sound of the door opening and closing. Then he was gone on our errand and the house was silent.

It wasn't until much later, after Daniel's two younger nieces were in bed, that the chill began to pass and I was almost able to forget what Daniel was doing. Even today, when I think of what went on, on that cold, dark night, I shudder.

Lin Sun didn't say anything for a long time after dinner, but her oldest daughter kept watching me out of the corner of her eye. There was something in her expression; I couldn't tell, maybe she was afraid of me and what I had brought to her house.

Lin Sun finally lit a fire in the cast-iron stove and pulled up chairs for the three of us. I don't think the night was really that cold, but I think we were all chilled anyway. Lin Sun brought in some green tea, and we sat in chairs in front of the stove holding our warm tea cups in our cold hands.

I was surprised when Lin Sun's oldest daughter, Hana, began speaking in English. Her English wasn't as good as Daniel's but it was still good.

"Daniel has helped me learn American," she explained, "but I was shy to talk in front of you. My mother, though wants me to help."

Lin Sun said something in Chinese and Hana slowly

translated it for me.

"Daniel is good brother," she said. Lin Sun continued talking and letting Hana translate.

"What he do is not good — not good at all. I no …" Hana struggled for the word while her mother waited, "blame. Maybe must be done. Don't know …" There was another pause as Lin Sun spoke to her. "Ancestors be displeased."

"I'm really sorry," I said.

"No sorry. Sometimes …" Lin Sun shrugged, but her voice became very soft. Hana continued translating "things must be done."

I lowered my head and nodded. Yes, sometimes things must be done.

We stayed up that night. I had no desire to sleep and when Hana rolled out a futon for me I just nodded and thanked her.

I don't know if Lin Sun and Hana stayed up out of politeness or because they were as nervous as I was, but none of us moved. Slowly, as the night grew colder, the walls between us seemed to lower and we began to talk, mostly about nothing. They didn't ask me much about the future. I don't think they wanted to know. There were also long periods of silence. I hope they found some comfort in my being there. It certainly helped me to be with them.

~~~ ~~~ ~~~

Shortly before 4:00 a.m., I knew Daniel had returned. I listened intently for a second and was rewarded by the sound of a creaking board on the porch and the squeak of the door opening.

Daniel was dirty and exhausted. He looked awful — and it wasn't just the dirt and exhaustion. He had a haunted look, jittery and nervous, and something else I couldn't understand. There was something in his eyes that puzzled me. At first I thought it was guilt for what he had done, but slowly I came to think that way back there, through the dirt, exhaustion and guilt was a hint of triumph. I waited for him to speak.

"I have found something," he said at last. "I'm not sure yet what it means, though."

"What, Daniel?" I asked. "What did you find?"

He closed his eyes and his body swayed. When he looked at me his eyes were unfocused. "Your mother is a veterinarian?" The words dragged out so slowly.

"Yes."

"That is good, but still I must think." He staggered to a side room. "We will talk in the morning when I can think through things and make sure about my thoughts."

In the morning! I wanted to know now so that I could … My mind raced. So I could what? What was I going to do even if Daniel had found the answer? How was I going to get back to my own time with whatever Daniel had found out. Something nagged at me, something Isabel had said. What was it?

Then I remembered. She said we were forgetting something, something about the time traveling. The stamp. The stamp! I needed to bring a stamp so I could get back.

I lay down on the mattress and closed my eyes. Even if Daniel learned something that could help my mom, how could I ever get it to her? For the first time, I began to think I might be stuck in 1894. Isabel had figured it out and tried to help me. That's why I'd heard her rummaging in her desk. She was looking for a canceled stamp from 1994 so I would have a way back just in case it worked.

I pushed my head further into the small pillow and started to cry. Isabel had tried so hard to make sure I could get back but she was too late. I must have cried for a half an hour, stifling my sobs so I wouldn't wake up the small household.

I opened my eyes to see Daniel's silhouette against a window that was starting to lighten with the new day. He was sitting on the floor by my mattress, looking tired but focused. As my eyes blinked open, he smiled. "I think I know now what killed my father. I hope information will be of use to your mother, though I do not know how."

I smiled and then I remembered and my smile fell. Suddenly I was crying again. Daniel stared at me in confusion.

"I can't get back home. I don't know how to travel in time."

"But I don't understand," Daniel said. "How could you be here now if you cannot travel …? What about stamp?"

"What about stamp?" I snapped and I immediately felt awful for mimicking this kind and wonderful man.

He stared at me, not responding to my cruelty.

"Daniel," I said, sobbing, "I forgot to bring a stamp to get back."

Daniel shook his head. "But that can't be."

"Well, it is."

"No, I mean it is too strange for you to come here at all. Surely the marvelous power that brought you here for your most pressing need will not abandon you now."

I looked at him and my tears stopped. "I don't understand."

"I don't either, but I know what we must do. We must search our minds for the answer."

I nodded. "Okay."

"All right, then. Tell me again how you did it, how you came back to our time."

I paused and thought.

"Well, it wasn't exactly our idea, we got it from someone else who lives in this time."

"But how?"

"It was in a historical library just like your father's diary. That's what my friend was looking at while I was reading your father's diary. The diary she read was about a stamp collector who explained how to travel in time by putting a stamp on your forehead and thinking about the time you wanted to go to."

Daniel closed his eyes and seemed to be thinking. After a few moments he opened his eyes.

"Just a stamp? That brought you back to us?"

I nodded. "I lay down on a bed with a candle on either side of my head and the moon shining in my face. Then I put the stamp on my forehead upside down and woke up at Ardenwood."

"You woke up at what?"

"Ardenwood — I mean at the Patterson Farm."

"But what is this Ardenwood?" Daniel asked.

"That's what they call the Patterson farm in my time."

"The Patterson farm? It is still there in your time?"

"Well, yes …" I said. "Of course it's a museum now."

Daniel was startled. "A museum? A farm is a museum?"

I nodded. "Yes. People go there to see what life was like back — well, back now."

"And you came here using a stamp?"

I shrugged my shoulders. "That's what we did."

"You and your friend?"

"She helped me, but now I don't have a stamp, not even the one I used."

"I have the stamp you used."

"How …?"

"After I helped with Nelly's birth, I went into room where you woke up. Henry brought me. He wanted to tell how everything happened. All others were watching new foal and there was no explaining needed. I was, of course, most curious about the girl who appeared from the future."

He stood up and lit a candle on a table near the window. Then he reached into his pants pocket.

"I found stamp on the pillow and was certain it was yours."

He held the stamp out to me and I took it.

"But I don't think this will work. Don't I need a stamp from my own time?"

"I don't think stamp brought you here. I think love for your mother did." He paused and shook his head. "Margie, I do not understand how you came to be here, but I trust very much you can go back."

"Why do you say that?"

"All things balance, Margie. The stamp will get you back. If not stamp, something will. You do not belong to us, to our time, and you will go back. I think you must merely believe and want it. That is all that is needed. Even the stamp, I think is not needed."

"You mean like Dorothy in the *Wizard of Oz?*"

Daniel looked at me and smiled. "More future talk, Margie? Yet you must believe in yourself, I think that is all."

I listened to his voice and felt his confidence enter me like the warmth of a fire. I closed my eyes and I knew he was right. All I needed was to think about home, about Isabel's bed, about her house and her room and the crucifix on the wall. I just needed to think about the details and I would go back to my own time, to Isabel's room, to my family. I opened my eyes for a moment and saw the candle. Then I closed them with the halo of candlelight still lighting the insides of my eyelids.

"Margie, not yet. I must tell you what …"

I opened my eyes and gasped when I saw the moon framed in the window over my head.

<　10　>

An Untimely Return

"Margie, wait, I need to get another stamp so you can get back."

"Isabel?" I blurted.

"What? Just wait a minute will you? We forgot that you'll need another stamp to get back."

I shivered. "No. Isabel," I said, sitting up on the bed, "I'm already back."

"What do you mean?"

"I went back to 1894 and now I'm back."

"Right, Margie. While I was looking through my desk drawer, you went on the greatest adventure in history. I always knew you were egotistical, but this beats all."

"But I did, Isabel. I met Daniel Lee and his family. Henry Patterson was there. Daniel worked at the Patterson farm."

Isabel looked at me blankly.

"Ardenwood Farm. I woke up there. Henry Patterson helped me and then he betrayed me."

"You mean like Judas betrayed Jesus?" Isabel said, laughing.

"Isabel, I went back in time, one hundred years."

Isabel smiled. "This is cute, Margie, very cute."

"But it happened, Isabel. Daniel and I took his wagon to Stockton. It took two days. And he talked his sister into letting him do the autopsy on his father."

Isabel came close to my bed. She had a puzzled expression. I think she was starting to believe me or at least to take me seriously. She stared at me for a long time and I stared back. Slowly, the challenging look disappeared from her eyes.

"What did he find out, Margie? That's what really matters. What's happening to your mother?"

"Oh no!" I shook my head. "I never found out. Daniel was about to tell me ..."

I burst into tears. The whole thing was wasted. I went back in time and didn't even learn anything to help my mother. It was as if it never happened.

I looked in Isabel's eyes again and knew that it hadn't happened. It had all been a stupid dream. It was still Sunday night and nothing had happened except in my mind. Here I was at Isabel's house and that meant one horrible thing was true.

"My mother is dying, isn't she?" I said. It was almost an accusation, but I felt so confused.

Isabel shook her head sadly. "Margie, I don't know. I'm sure everything will ..." Her voice trailed off.

"But Daniel found out ..." I shook my head. Daniel had died decades ago. I must have dreamt he did an autopsy. Slowly I got up from the bed.

"What am I going to do?"

Isabel didn't say anything and I started pacing. I jammed my hand in my pocket and felt a scrap of paper. I pulled it out. It was the fortune from the Chinese restaurant, the place where this horror story all started. Was it all some kind of food poisoning? If we'd gone to Zachary's for pizza would my mom still be all right?

I glared at the two Chinese characters; then let it drop to the floor.

I walked to the window and stared up at the moon, remembering the dew-covered grass and the quilt. "I did go back, Isabel." I felt tears dripping from my eyes. "I went back and Daniel found out something. He's still trying to tell me something. There's something I'm missing."

Isabel looked at me with hopeless confusion

"'All things in balance,' Isabel. That's what Daniel told me and I think he meant that I was destined to go back in time and find the answer and there was no way I could mess it up because it had to happen. I just have to figure it out."

Isabel's hand reached the doorknob and she was suddenly out of the room.

I didn't care, I kept pacing and talking, now to myself.

"I went back and I changed history. I know I did. Daniel didn't do the autopsy originally, but then he did it because I went back. So something changed because of me." I paused. "But how is that going to help my mom?"

Isabel had returned with Mr. and Mrs. Molina. Isabel looked upset. Her parents looked confused and tired. I looked at the clock; it was only ten minutes after midnight. Mr. Molina glanced around the room, at the bed by the window and the candles. "What's happening here?" he asked.

"I don't know," Isabel said. "Margie put a stamp on her forehead and the next thing she started talking about having gone back in time."

Mrs. Molina came over and put her arm around my shoulder.

"It's okay, sweetheart. Everything is okay."

I looked at her, but my eyes didn't quite focus. I felt like I was looking through her to the wallpaper behind.

"I know it's okay, Mrs. Molina. I mean I hope so. I think it is. I think it will be okay. I just need to figure it out."

"You can't take responsibility for your mother's illness. You are only a girl. No one expects you to be able to save her." Her voice was soothing and soft, but the words just went right through me.

"I didn't go back in time, did I?" I said suddenly. It didn't really matter anyway. I hadn't learned anything.

Mr. Molina put a hand on my arm. "Of course not, Margie. It isn't possible." I pulled my arm away, not wanting him to comfort me.

I closed my eyes, listening to Mr. and Mrs. Molina move the bed back. "I guess I just wanted to so badly, to find out …" I couldn't finish the sentence.

~~~ ~~~ ~~~

Mr. and Mrs. Molina left Isabel's room soon after. Before she left, Mrs. Molina made us promise to get to sleep right away, but I couldn't help talking. I didn't want it all to slip away from me. It seemed like so much more than a dream and I kept thinking there was something more in it that I would find if I could just hold onto it, just tell it to someone. Isabel, as curious as she was, was tired. She asked a few questions as I talked and said "u-huh" a few times in an increasingly tired voice. Then I was alone, staring at the window and wondering. What had really happened and what did it have to do with my mother?

~~~ ~~~ ~~~

I somehow beat Isabel to third period on Monday. English Composition had already started when she arrived. I was seated, and per instructions, working on free writing. The classroom was silent except for the scratching of pencils and pens, the gritty shuffle of feet on the worn linoleum floor, and the sound of Isabel's footsteps coming through the door. I looked up to see her come in. Mrs. Conger looked too, and seeing it was Isabel, she quickly looked at me, mouthing the words: "keep writing."

I turned back to my paper, but I wasn't writing. I was

staring at the paper, thinking of nothing at all. My mind had never been so blank, but it was like this noise of voices going on in another room of my brain. Everything had gotten so slippery and gray. What had last night meant?

⌇⌇⌇ ⌇⌇⌇ ⌇⌇⌇

Isabel grabbed me in the hallway after class. "I had this dream about a dream last night," she told me.

"Riddles!" I said, exasperated. "Spit it out. I have to get to class."

"I dreamt about Jonah last night."

"You can't dream about Jonah. Didn't we agree not to talk about him?" I said. I didn't really care. I didn't care about anything, but I found myself responding out of habit.

"Yes," Isabel said. "We agreed not to talk to him … but I can't help what I dream, you know."

"Okay," I said. "You made your point." I paused. "What did you dream?"

"I dreamed he wanted to go see a movie."

"And he asked you to go with him?"

"No, he asked you." She scowled. "Talk about a raw deal — and in my own dream. I don't want you using my dreams anymore."

I shook my head.

"And I thought dreams were supposed to be wish fulfillment. Even my own dreams turn against me. I could have had a romantic, sexy dream, but no, I had to have this stupid dream where the object of my lust asks you out. Go figure."

"My grandmother used to say 'go figure.' Only old Jewish ladies say 'go figure.'"

"Yeah?" Isabel said quickly. "See, even my language isn't my own." She suddenly looked at her watch. "Say, aren't you going to be late for your next period?" She gave me a push down the hall toward the ramp. My next class was up the ramp, down the hall to the right and the last room on the left. She stepped across the hall and through the doorway into her class.

"Hurry!" she said. "You'll be late for class. And no talking to Jonah, understood?"

At that moment, the bell rang and I was off.

~~~ ~~~ ~~~

At lunchtime I called home. I hadn't seen mom and dad since Thursday morning when I'd found them sleeping. I pulled one of my two emergency phone call quarters out of my backpack and put it in the pay phone across from the school office. Mrs. Snow watched me through the glass panel like she was a store detective and I was a teenage boy in the lingerie department. The principal probably told her to look out for kids "abusing" their telephone privileges or something.

Dad answered after three rings, just as the answering machine was starting its message. We both waited for it to end.

"How is Mom?"

"Margie?" he said, clearly confused. I wondered what he'd been doing and thinking before the phone rang. Maybe he was waiting for someone else to call.

"I didn't expect you to call," he said after a second. "Aren't you supposed to be in class?"

"It's lunch time. How's Mom doing?"

"She's nesting. She's …" I waited, but he didn't continue.

"Dad, we can't just let her get sicker."

"I know, Margie. I called Dr. Albers again, you remember, the specialist down in Palo Alto. I'm waiting for her to call back."

"Can I talk to Mom?" I asked.

"She's sleeping right now. Is there something you want

me to tell her when she gets up?"

I sighed. "No, that's okay. I'll see you when I get home."

I hung up the phone and turned around. Mrs. Snow was standing by her desk, staring at me. As I started down the hall to class, she waved and I stopped, surprised. I'd never seen her wave at anyone before.

⌇⌇⌇ ⌇⌇⌇ ⌇⌇⌇

Mrs. Molina picked both of us up unexpectedly right after school. At least I didn't expect it. I think Isabel knew but forgot. Isabel needed dress shoes and Mrs. Molina asked if I wanted a ride home.

When Mrs. Molina dropped me off, I went straight around back to Mom's clinic hoping to find her back at work, but the door was locked and the sign still said "closed." I'd expected it, still it was easy to hope she'd be out wearing her lab coat and pulling porcupine quills out of a terrier's nose or bandaging a footpad on a beloved calico cat. I was startled to hear my dad's voice through the kitchen window. I stopped in my tracks.

"I don't know what to tell her."

Mom's voice was light and breathy when she answered.

"The truth, Neil. We always have to tell her the truth."

"Well," her father's voiced started, "of course we'll tell her the truth, but we don't want her to worry any more than she is now."

"I don't think she could worry any more than she is now, Neil. She's keeping it all inside, but I think she's nearly out of her mind with worry."

"She'll be home in a few minutes," Dad said.

I started to walk around to the front door so I could come in normally and interrupt their conversation, but I was walking slowly, dragging my feet. Finally I turned and crept back to the door, my ears wide open to listen as they talked about how little the doctors knew and how scared they were.

I couldn't get to sleep that night. My mind kept replaying what I'd overheard standing outside the kitchen and the more cautious family discussion we had later in the living room after dinner. Maybe I did get to sleep. If I did, I dreamed I was awake, overhearing the one conversation where Mom and Dad talked *about* me and the worse one where they talked *to* me and nobody really said anything at all. Their empty reassurances were so much more frightening than facts.

Tuesday morning I woke at 6:45 and got right out of bed. I knew Mom wouldn't be giving me a wake-up call.

Dad met me in the kitchen and told me Mom was sleeping in. When I went into her room to say good morning, she was propped up on several pillows like a princess. The curtains were still closed and it was dark. She was sleeping. It wasn't until I got close that I saw her face, how drawn and pale it was. It didn't look like her at all. I gasped and ran from the room. Dad was standing at the door as I ran out of the room, out of the house, not stopping until I was halfway down the block.

I barely remember Wednesday. I avoided Mom's room and Dad seemed to avoid me. I think he was staying up with her at night and was too tired to put on a happy face. I felt like I was alone in the house. I made my own breakfast and lunch and I made dinner for all three of us when I got home from school. Dad came out for dinner and we had very careful conversations that didn't say anything at all about Mom. Dad took a plate to her up in the room. Both Tuesday and Wednesday nights I found what looked like the whole dinner in the garbage afterward.

Following dinner those nights Dad sat with Mom. I spent some time there too, but I couldn't stay long. The room smelled sick and I felt cooped up, frightened, and dizzy when I was in there. I didn't see Dad again until I had gone to bed and the lights were out. Then he came into the room and said "sweet dreams." Can you imagine anything more bizarre than saying "sweet dreams" with Mom lying there so sick just down the hall.

Before he left I asked why mom wasn't in the hospital. He told me she'd wanted to stay home, to be around me, but that she was so tired it wasn't making any sense to be home. The doctor was anxious to get her checked into the hospital. He said he'd be making the arrangements today.

My dreams *were* sweet, that night. I dreamt I hadn't come back too early and I'd been there long enough for Daniel Lee to tell me what he'd found out. Like most dreams what he said was nonsense. I woke up thinking about my fortune, wondering what I'd done with it.

On Thursday I went home with Isabel after school. That was Mom's idea. I was relieved, but I felt guilty not going home, not putting in my useless time in that depressing place. It was my duty to worry about Mom and feel sorry for myself.

I tried not to think about Mom or Dad or what was going on. Everything was falling apart. Dad wasn't working on any of his construction projects. His carpenters were keeping things going, but it sounded like there were problems, and he wasn't doing anything about them. Mom's clinic had been closed since my birthday and I couldn't do anything to help. I felt as useful as a bicycle to a fish.

I was sitting at Isabel's desk staring at my report outline and feeling sorry for myself when Isabel brought up Jonah again. I think she was trying to pull me out of my dark mood.

"I think you're the one he's interested in," Isabel said, flopping on the bed.

"Who cares?" I asked, and I meant it. How could I care about some stupid boy with my mom so sick?

"I care," Isabel said stridently. "He's the cutest boy in the school."

I shrugged my shoulders and let my eyes wander up the wall to where her gruesome crucifix hung on the wall. Jesus looked so pained, his head twisted to one side and blood oozing out of the holes in his arms and legs.

"What's with you Catholics, anyway?" I blurted out.

"What …?" Isabel asked.

"Why do you worship an image of a man in torment on a cross?"

Isabel shook her head slowly from side to side. I don't think she knew where I was coming from. Why should she? I didn't even know where I was coming from. She waited and I waited. For a long time, her room was very quiet.

"We don't worship an image and we don't worship the cross. We worship the man who gave his life for us."

"I know," I said. "You don't need to tell me, again."

"Then why did you …?" Isabel started, but she stopped. I was upset about my mother and Isabel knew it well enough. Still, I realized I'd hurt her when I said that. Neither of us said anything for a long time.

Finally, the silence became too loud and I had to break it. I meant to say 'I'm sorry." I thought the words and felt them forming on my tongue, but when I opened my mouth that's not what came out.

"My mom is dying," I said. I stared at Isabel's face and felt my eyes get hot. Then my tears started. "I love her," I said, but that wasn't what I meant to say either. What I meant to say was that I needed her.

Isabel sat beside me on the bed and held my head against her shoulder and I thought it was exactly what my mother would have done.

I think we were both relieved when Mrs. Molina called us down to dinner. Isabel called out that we would be down in a minute. I took the time to pull myself together.

As we took our places at the table, Mrs. Molina asked about our homework.

"We're going to do it after dinner, Mom."

"Do you always put off your homework, Margie?" Mrs. Molina asked.

I glanced at Isabel and opened my mouth to answer, but Mr. Molina interrupted.

"They need some time to unwind after a day in school." He said. "They've been listening attentively, studying hard, and turning away the advances of the boys. Am I right, girls?"

Isabel nodded. "Absolutely, Dad," She winked broadly at all of us.

Mrs. Molina laughed. "Okay, you win, but I want you to get your homework done right after you do the dishes. All right?" By 'you' Mrs. Molina meant both of us. I was pretty much an accepted member of the family when I was there, with all the rights and responsibilities that went with that. We agreed, but Isabel was grumbling. If it had been my house, I would have grumbled.

"So how's that new boy in class? Jonah? Is that his name?" Mr. Molina asked.

I looked at Isabel in surprise. I had never spoken about Jonah in my house. I felt like my interest in boys (as little as there was) was my secret and I didn't want it opened for family discussion. I was shocked that Isabel had told her parents about him. She looked at me and shrugged.

"He's okay. I guess," Isabel said without much expression. Her father nodded, knowingly, as if he understood a lot more than Isabel had said. Then he turned to me.

"Well, how about you, Margie? Isabel says this Jonah is Jewish so maybe he'd be interested in a beautiful Jewish girl like you."

I blushed and Mrs. Molina interrupted. "Now, Alex, this is none of your business. Let the girls have their own lives."

"You misunderstand me. It's just my Spanish blood. You know we are all incurable romantics. And someone has to fan the flames of passion."

"There will be no fanning the flames of passion around here," Mrs. Molina said sternly, but with a hint of laughter in her voice. She mouthed something to Mr. Molina that looked like "at least not now." Then she sent us to the kitchen and the dishes.

For a while, Isabel was embarrassed and didn't say much, but later on, when we were doing our homework she loosened up and we were able to have a normal conversation again. By the time I had to go home, we had returned to talking about Jonah.

My dad had said he was going to pick me up, so I was surprised when Mrs. Molina said she was going to walk me home.

The living room was dark. I found Dad in the kitchen, drinking coffee. He didn't even look up at first. Finally he looked up and met my eyes. He nodded and almost smiled. The house smelled sick.

"Mom's in bed," he said softly.

"How is she?" I asked, though I knew the answer. He shrugged, more out of resignation than anything else.

"Well, she's really tired," he said. "She says she's sick of being sick." He gave a look like we were sharing some big joke, but he didn't convince me or himself. "We're going down to Palo Alto tomorrow to check into the hospital. This is it, the heavy guns. They're going to keep her under the bright lights until they figure out what's going on. Up to now, Mom's resisted it. She wanted to stay at home if she could to keep things normal, but now we're going to make sure they test every possibility."

"She's had a lot of tests," I said angrily. "It's not going to help. Nothing is."

Dad nodded. "It's been tough on all of us, and I guess it must be worse for you, getting everything second hand. We should have kept you more involved when mom went to the doctors, let you hear everything from the horse's mouth. We were trying to do what was best, but I guess we blew it. Instead of protecting you, we've cut you out. I'm sorry. But I'm sure we'll find out what's going on soon. The doctors will be able to stay focused on mom in the hospital."

"They don't know anything," I said loudly. "They don't know *anything*."

He nodded, agreeing, but reluctantly. "They'll find something soon, Margie — and the best thing you and I can do for Mom is to be strong and supportive and let the doctors do what they do best."

I shook my head. More doctors, more theories, more dead ends. Why couldn't they find out what was wrong with her?

"What time are we leaving?" I asked.

Dad looked down at the coffee. "Only mom and I are going."

"What?"

"We'll be there for several days at least, Margie, and you have school."

I tried to interrupt, but he stopped me. "I talked to Monica and Alejandro. They said you could stay with them." He paused. "It won't be too long, and you'll be with Isabel."

"But what about …?" I yelled, but Dad held up his hand.

"Don't wake Mom. She needs her sleep."

"That's all she does." I said it just like that, as if she were doing it just to hurt me. Then I felt absolutely awful.

"Margie …"

"I'm sorry," I said bitterly. "But what's the point of me staying in school? I can't concentrate anyway."

"It's your job to finish out your year of school — and prepare for your Bat Mitzvah. Mine is to go with Mom and make sure the doctors and nurses take good care of her."

I sat down heavily in a chair.

"When are *you* leaving?"

"Tomorrow morning at 9:00 a.m. Doctor Albers wants to see Mom at the clinic at 10:30. She's coming in on her day off just to see her."

His expression was so calm, almost reassuring. He looked more confident than I'd seen him in days, but it didn't help me. I was beginning to think I was the only one who could have helped and I'd let her down.

Mrs. Molina showed up promptly at eight Friday morning to stay with Mom while Dad drove me to school. I was in Mom's room trying to keep my spirits up so I wouldn't make her feel any worse, while Dad ran around packing bags and getting the last-minute things together.

Mom could see how I was feeling — maybe more than I could. She was telling me all those reassuring mom things: how I had to be good for Mrs. Molina; the importance of education; and how advanced science was. It all sounded so trite, but the tone of her voice was soothing and reassuring. When Dad came to get me, I kissed Mom and she gave me a weak hug.

I followed Dad to the door. When I turned around Mom's eyes were already closed and she seemed to be all but swallowed by the shadows in the room.

Mrs. Molina met me at the top of the stairs and put her arm around my shoulders to prop me up on the way down.

"She'll be all right," Mrs. Molina said. "She's like you, Margie. She's a fighter — and fighters survive. And she has all of us fighting for her." I wanted to ask what we were doing for her, how we were helping, but I kept quiet. Mrs. Molina squeezed my shoulder. "Come. You must go now with your father."

I got into the car and sat without looking at Dad. He started the car and drove down Hillegass toward school.

"I don't understand," I said as dad waited for the traffic to let up at Ashby Avenue.

"I don't either. It's all so confoundedly mysterious. But I'm confident in Dr. Albers."

"I didn't mean that, what I meant was why are you driving me to school? Why don't you just let me walk to school like usual and whisk Mom away while I'm gone? I'm not part of this family anymore."

I gave him a challenging look, but he was watching the road and couldn't see the hardness in my eyes.

"It's more complicated than you think. I was tempted to take you out of school and bring you with us to Palo Alto."

"And …?"

"Okay, Margie. I'm going to tell you the difficult part. I'm asking you to do the hardest thing I've ever asked you to do. That's why I'm driving you to school. I needed time to talk about this where Mom couldn't hear."

"Talk about what?" I asked, now angry, confused and curious.

"Your mom wants you to be with her more than anything. She begged me to let you come along."

"But then why didn't …"

"Wait a minute. Do you know why she wants you to come along?"

"Of course. I'm her daughter."

"That's right, but there's more. Your mom thinks she's going to die and she wants you to be there, so she can say good-bye."

Dad had stopped in front of the school. Kids were all around the car and I was suddenly crying like a baby. "She's going to die and I'm not going to be there?"

Dad was crying, too, but he kept talking through the tears.

"We can't let her give up, Margie. We have to convince her she can beat this and that we believe she will. Otherwise she'll give up. That's why I don't want you in Palo Alto. I don't want to make it easier for her to give up. I want her to keep fighting until Dr. Albers can find an answer. Do you understand?"

"Understand? How can I understand something like that?" I yelled. "No, I don't understand and I don't want to."

I opened the car door and ran out, pushing my way through the other kids as they poured into the school courtyard. At the gate, I turned to see him pulling away from the curb. I did understand — and I hated him for being right.

⌁⌁⌁ ⌁⌁⌁ ⌁⌁⌁

I was at Isabel's again Friday, but her house, which had been a refuge for me, wasn't anymore. I didn't want to be with anyone, didn't have anything to say — and I felt that if I started talking, I wouldn't be able to stop. I would ramble and babble and finally cry and I needed so much not to start crying.

I disappeared into Isabel's room as soon as I got home and Isabel, who practically lived in her room on normal days, left me alone.

I lay on Isabel's extra bed, now my bed, hearing dinner being prepared, footsteps in the hallway, water running in the bathroom. I smelled dinner and when Isabel knocked on the door I just said, "No, thank you." My brain swam with images of my mom, exaggerated images of her face, thinning as she ate less and less, colorless, pained and confused, her eyes looking at me without focusing.

I closed my eyes tightly to block it out and started to sweat. I shivered uncontrollably. I pulled the edge of the bedspread up over me, sliding across the bed until there was enough to cover me.

This time, when I closed my eyes, I got a clear image

110

of a funeral, my mom's funeral. I saw myself watching. I could see I was sick; that nausea was overcoming me. I opened my eyes and my stomach felt knotted. The room was sliding sideways. I felt like I was about to throw up. Carefully, I pulled myself to a sitting position, fighting the nausea, and getting ready to run to the bathroom.

Sitting seemed to help. I focused my eye on the clock by Isabel's bed and the room steadied and my stomach started to relax, but the clock seemed too clear, too much in focus. As I looked around the room, I saw that everything was in brighter colors and sharper focus than I'd ever seen before. Even the pattern on Isabel's bedspread suddenly stood out. The flowers looked like they were bouquets, lying there in bunches, and on the floor, just under the edge of Isabel's bed was a bright spot of white, the corner of a small scrap of paper.

It struck me that the paper was somehow important. I stood up and took the two steps, feeling like I was going a long distance, very quickly. As I picked up the paper and began to straighten up, the Chinese characters jumped out at me. It was my fortune from my birthday dinner. I turned it over and looked at it. On the back, carefully printed, were the words 'Believe in Yourself.'

My head started spinning again, only this time in confusion. I heard footsteps on the stairs and then in the hall. There was a knock on the door and Mrs. Molina's voice came through. "Margie, can I come in?"

I didn't answer. I just stared at the dark letters on the bright, white background. I couldn't answer.

"Margie?" she asked, concern coloring her voice.

I stared at the letters, knowing they were important, but unable to figure out why.

I heard the knob turn and looked up at Mrs. Molina. Our eyes met and I saw her expression of concern turn to something else, confusion or …

I looked at the fortune, then handed it to Mrs. Molina. Isabel and Mr. Molina stepped into the room and watched as she turned it over and looked. They all looked at the Chinese characters and then read the English as Mrs. Molina turned it over.

"Margie?" she asked.

"It's my fortune," I said, realizing how dumb that must have sounded. "I got it on my birthday night."

"It's a great fortune, Margie," Mr. Molina said carefully. "Believe in yourself."

I smiled, realizing that they didn't know — that they didn't understand.

"I saved you some dinner, Margie. You need to eat."

"Mr. Lee translated it for me," I said.

Mr. and Mrs. Molina nodded, still not understanding, but I watched Isabel as the words sank in.

"Mr. Lee?" She asked.

Mrs. Molina looked from Isabel to me. "I don't understand," she said.

Isabel turned to her mother. "It was in the diary — the one Margie read."

"This is about the diary?" Mr. Molina asked.

I nodded again. "Don't you see? I did go back in time. Otherwise how could Mr. Lee have translated it."

"But I don't understand," Mr. Molina said. "You know you didn't travel in time."

"There's more," I said. "There must be something more, something I overlooked. My fortune said 'believe in yourself' and then I didn't believe. I went back in time and then I thought I must have dreamed the whole thing, but the fortune proves it actually happened. I did go back in time." I walked to the window and looked out, trying to find the missing piece. I turned around as Mr. and Mrs. Molina exchanged a concerned look.

"It was that history report," Mrs. Molina whispered. "She shouldn't have had to do it. It was too much additional stress. She had too much on her mind, already."

She thought I couldn't hear, but I heard everything as if she were whispering in my ear.

"Then that diary started her off," Isabel said.

"The diary!" I said suddenly.

Isabel looked back at me. "What about the diary?"

"He stopped writing in it right after his father died," I said it like I was talking to little children, "and when I saw it on his desk in his house, it was right on the last page he'd written."

Isabel shook her head and I smiled.

"But don't you see? Daniel could have gone back home and written in it. He would have written in it, wouldn't he? He would have written down what he found out, because he knew I had it or could get it. I told him I'd read about his father in it and he'd figure this was a way to communicate with me." I paused remembering that conversation with Daniel just before I went to bed. "He said it was good that Mom was a veterinarian, like that explained something. Her sickness must have something to do with working with animals."

Slowly Mrs. Molina got up and looked around the room.

"What diary is she talking about, Isabel?"

"Well, she, I mean we took … borrowed a diary from Mrs. Snyder's library, for our report."

"Victoria never lets anyone 'borrow' anything. They aren't replaccable," Mrs. Molina said angrily.

Isabel shrugged. "Mom …"

"Well, where is it?"

"It's on my desk, Mom. It's under the dictionary."

I watched as Mrs. Molina lifted up the papers and carefully turned over page after page. My breathing stopped, my heartbeat slowed and I prayed in my head that she would find the new pages that had to be there. I realized I was holding my breath.

She moved so slowly that my head started feeling light and the room began to darken. I told myself to breathe while I watched Mrs. Molina's face.

"Dios mio," she said finally and I gasped for air. "He

says he found some kind of parasite in the brain tissue of his father with his microscope. 'A tiny worm,' he calls it. He mentions a raccoon that scratched his father some time before he became ill." She lifted her head to look at me.

I realized my head was nodding, as if the nodding motion made it easier for me to process what I was hearing.

"Mom was scratched by a raccoon." I said, flatly, my voice coming from somewhere else. "On her hand. It was infected, but then it cleared up."

Mrs. Molina turned to me her eyes wide and her mouth open. "I remember," she said. "Yes, a raccoon."

I stared and nodded. Mom had told all of us about going under the house to get out the cat and meeting up with a raccoon.

"And this wasn't in the diary before …?"

I shook my head.

"Alejandro, call Margie's father. The number is downstairs on the refrigerator."

"But it's nine o'clock! The doctors aren't going to be on duty."

"I don't care what time it is. Call him."

He nodded. "Yes, of course." Then he disappeared out the door and was back almost immediately with a cordless phone.

I watched as he dialed the phone and I took it when he handed it to me.

Dad answered after three rings and I could tell by his voice that he was exhausted.

"Dad," I said.

"What, Margie? Why are you calling?"

"You have to talk to the doctor right away. Tell her that Mom was scratched by a raccoon, remember? She might have a parasite — maybe from a raccoon."

"But, Margie, what does that have to do with it? What makes you think …?" His voice trailed off.

"Dad, if I tried to explain it wouldn't help. Promise

me you will call the doctor right away and make sure you get through to her. You can't wait, you mustn't …"

"Okay, Margie. I'll call right now. Then I'll go over to the hospital and I will make sure they check this out."

"Do it right now."

"Okay, Margie. You know how much we love you."

"I know."

When I hung up, the Molina family was staring at me as if I was from Venus or something. Mrs. Molina was the first to speak.

"Well, I don't know anything about traveling in time, but I do know that growing girls need to eat. Do you think you could stand some dinner now?"

"Yes," I said, suddenly very hungry.

﹏﹏ ﹏﹏ ﹏﹏

The Molinas joined me at the table to keep me company. No one said much at first. I certainly didn't. I was too busy eating. Isabel broke the silence.

"This is going to make a great report, Margie."

"Report?" I asked.

"For Mr. Boylan. I mean, actually going back into history. That's way more than he expected."

Mrs. Molina laughed. "That's true, but who's going to believe it?"

I thought about that for a second. "I guess it doesn't matter who believes it." All that mattered was what happened down there in Palo Alto. Would what I told them help my mom? Was it the right answer? And even if it was the right answer, did I find it soon enough?

﹏﹏ ﹏﹏ ﹏﹏

After dinner, Isabel and I went up to bed. I felt too energized to get to sleep — at least until my head hit the pillow. I was out before the lights were, and Isabel had to shake me awake in the morning — which seemed to come a minute or two after I fell asleep.

"Margie, wake up. Your dad's on the phone."

I opened my eyes and looked around. For a second I couldn't remember what I was doing at Isabel's. She held the phone out to me.

"He's waiting to talk to you."

I picked up the phone and stared at it before I could bring it to my ear, and then I didn't say anything. I listened to the hiss of the line and my father's breathing.

"Margie?" he asked finally, "are you there?"

Still I couldn't talk.

"Margie?"

"Yes, Dad."

"Margie, what made you think there might be parasites?"

"Were there? Did they test her?"

"They took some tissue samples last night. It was a very delicate operation."

I felt my throat tighten. "Was I right?" The words squeaked out.

"We don't know yet, Margie. The lab is looking at the samples and we expect to hear later today. Dr. Albers spoke to some other doctors this morning, doctors who know more about animal parasites. They confirmed that her symptoms match what they would expect from a parasitic infection of the nervous system. The doctor started Mom on medication immediately after I spoke to her."

"You mean before they got the results of the tests?"

"Yes. They started the medication at 9:30 last night — they said that time was critical."

I thought about what he'd said. I guessed that I would never hear an expression about time again without wondering about it.

"Keep your fingers crossed, Margie," Dad said.

"Don't worry. They've been crossed so long, I think

they're broken."

There was a long silence on the line.

"Dad?"

"Yes?"

I couldn't think of anything to say.

"I'm going to go back to Mom's room now. As soon as I hear the test results I'll call you." There was a pause on the line. "Someday you'll explain this to me, all right?"

"All right, Dad. Kiss Mom for me."

<　11　>

THE CIRCLE CLOSES

After that I was jittery waiting to hear, waiting for the phone to ring. I told the whole story to the Molinas over breakfast. They listened closely, but the looks they gave me … it was clear they didn't know what to think about my story or about the entries in the diary. They seemed ready to admit something weird had happened, but not ready to accept what I told them.

"Well, I don't understand it at all. How did the new entries get into the diary?" Mrs. Molina said.

"But it's obvious!" I said. "Daniel Lee wrote them after I left."

Mr. Molina shook his head slowly, trying to fathom what I was saying. "But you didn't go anywhere, and the diary was here the whole time."

I thought about that and nodded. "I guess I didn't go anywhere. I mean Isabel was with me the whole time in the room, so I couldn't have. Still, I spent almost three days in 1894 with some very nice people who are all …"

I hesitated, then continued softly, "I guess … I guess they're all dead." I shook my head. "They've been dead a long time."

The Molinas were staring at me.

"You must understand how hard this is for us to … to accept." That was Mr. Molina.

I smiled. "That's okay. I have a hard time accepting it. Still, I think Mr. Lee was right — it had to happen. I needed to go back there in order to help my mother … I only hope I have helped."

It surprised me that I didn't care what Isabel's family believed. I saw them as wonderful, caring people who couldn't figure out what was going on. Well, big deal! I couldn't figure it out either.

〜〜 〜〜 〜〜

I was reading Daniel Lee's new diary entries when Isabel came into the room an hour later. He had started writing in his diary a few days after we went to Stockton and what I read gave me shivers. He never mentioned me by name. I guess I expected to see my name written down there in big red letters or something. I re-read the entry from the morning that I came back:

> **September 10:** *I have had a wondrous visitor, but now she is gone. I wanted much to help her, but she left so quick. I wanted her to know what killed father. She had such a pressing need. I would not have done autopsy but for her.*
>
> *Maybe I am not really good for a doctor. I can't even talk about my awful task. Yet I found strange things with nerves and darkened places on tissues of the brain stem. In my microscope, I saw tiny worms that should not have been in brain. I suddenly remember what father wrote about raccoon bite and then I understand why his hand never healed up right. Something from the raccoon got into him.*
>
> *It was difficult the next day. Visitor suddenly gone and my sister would not talk to me. I know these wounds heal*

eventually and we will be close again, but like father's death, this will be part of us from now on and it will always be there between us.

September 12: *I visit with Pattersons today. New foal is doing fine. It seem that Henry is finally forgiven. I now tell Henry I must deny knowing about visitor, but sometimes he and I talk about her. It is a strange secret we share.*

I had not planned to continue journal, but now feel very important to keep writing. I put this away as I planned before and will start new one. I try to think of where to keep this new journal so it is not lost to time. Then I think that I maybe cannot choose a wrong place, that wherever I put it, it will be found.

I could imagine Daniel Lee sitting at his small desk, an oil lamp casting shadows across the paper. I could almost hear his voice and glimpse his calm face and knew that, as he scribbled his journal entries, he was thinking about balance. I thought to myself about how the world was so carefully balanced and how somehow I had been allowed to tip the balance just this one time.

〰〰 〰〰 〰〰

Isabel and I spent most of Sunday working on my report, talking and planning, me retelling pieces of the story, trying to get it down as well as I could. Isabel was the first to suggest I write a book based on the report. We talked about it a lot. It was an exciting idea, but the first thing I wanted to do was get the outline ready for Tuesday and, between meals and walks and one small shopping trip, we got a lot done. By bedtime, I was feeling very good about the report. It was creative and interesting and I had a feel for the subject that I couldn't have gotten just from reading books — not even from original sources.

Dad called shortly after we turned the lights out. The doctors had found the parasites just like Mr. Lee had said and they spent Sunday assessing Mom's condition. They were excited because she responded immediately to the treatment and was already getting better. Mom was going to stay another couple days for observation and to begin physical therapy. They planned to return home on Wednesday morning. I should have been relieved, but now I shifted my worrying to how much damage had already been done, and what Mom would be like when she came home.

~~ ~~ ~~

Mrs. Molina sent us to visit Mrs. Snyder after breakfast on Labor Day. Mrs. Snyder had called earlier requesting that Isabel and I return for another visit.

"She is so diplomatic," Mrs. Molina said. "She didn't even mention the missing diary, but it was clear what she wanted." Mrs. Molina tried to give me a judgmental look, but it didn't take. In the end she smiled.

"I don't know what possessed you to take the diary, Margie, or how *you* …" she said, looking at Isabel, "could have let her do it." Isabel began to protest, but Mrs. Molina cut her off. "Anyway, it appears the diary was much more than a historical document."

~~ ~~ ~~

Just before noon, Isabel and I got off the bus and, after a few blocks on foot, found ourselves looking up the stairs to Mrs. Snyder's house. I climbed to the door with the diary in a manila envelope under one arm and my mouth full of apologies. When we reached the landing, the door swung in before us. Mrs. Snyder's granddaughter smiled and invited us to sit down in the living room. I set the envelope on the oak coffee table pushing it gently away from me. I pulled my hand back quickly when I heard Mrs. Snyder come in and glanced up at her.

She nodded her head toward the kitchen and her granddaughter disappeared through the door, emerging a moment later with a teapot and three cups on a silver tray. She set the tray on the table. Then she left the room. It seemed like she was in a hurry to get away from us.

Mrs. Snyder thanked her niece and turned back to us. She worked her way into the room using a cane and the back of a chair for support. Finally, defying gravity, she lowered herself into a crushed-velvet chair and settled in. Her fingers located some ornamental brass tacks on the arms of the chair and then she was ready for us.

I inhaled, ready to start my apology, but Mrs. Snyder spoke first.

"Well, I am glad to see three old friends returning."

I looked at her, then at Isabel.

"Of course I'm referring to the two of you — and the diary. In more than fifteen years it is the only document from the collection that has left this house." She nodded to the envelope on the table.

"I'm truly sorry, Mrs. Snyder. I don't know what came over me."

Mrs. Snyder smiled and held up her hand to silence me. "I understand from Mrs. Molina that something very profound came over you."

I nodded.

"When I called your mother this morning," she said to Isabel, "she told me about the strange events taking place in your house." She looked at me again. "She was not specific, although she did make some strange references to the diary. She said you two might elaborate."

I nodded slowly, then began telling her about what had happened and about Mrs. Molina's discovery.

She leaned forward and reverently picked up the envelope from the coffee table as I spoke, drawing out the yellowed papers. She listened without reaction as I told the story, only nodding and pursing her lips as if concentrating.

"As it happens," she said when I'd finished, "the Lee diary is one of my favorites. I've read it several times and am always fascinated by it. And, although I have found new revelations in the text with each reading, the text itself has not changed."

Mrs. Snyder turned through the pages to the back of the document.

"Monica did mention to me that I might find something very interesting at the end."

I watched as she paged through, imagining for a moment that there would be no new pages, but I saw her eyes grow wide as she began to read. After a minute she let her hands drop to her lap and stared off over our heads. Slowly she turned to look at me.

"Well, girls, Shakespeare once said that there is nothing new under the sun. Yet here we have something that is a hundred years old and yet is new."

She set the manuscript aside and looked at the two of us.

"I'm an old lady and my eyesight is beginning to deteriorate. I know that I will truly miss my friends, my books, when they become no more to me than brittle paper, yet I am thankful my eyes held out long enough to behold this. I truly thought I had seen about all there was to see. But last night and today have proven me mistaken."

"Last night?" Isabel and I asked at almost the same time.

"Yes, I woke up just before midnight with a strange feeling about the diary. Waking up at around midnight is, unfortunately, commonplace for me, but I rarely have concerns about my collection. In fact, I had suspected you were 'borrowing' one when you left that day, but I put it out of my mind. I knew you two were too honest to keep something that was not yours — and that you would take good care of it. More than that, I somehow knew there was a greater plan at work.

"In any event, I found myself suddenly sitting up in bed and wondering about the diary. I immediately had to go up and check things out.

"When I reached the room I noticed immediately that the manuscript was missing. But as I said, I half expected that. What surprised me was the envelope in its place."

"Envelope?" I asked. "I didn't leave an envelope."

"No, dear, it wasn't from you. Yet it was an envelope I had not seen before. In it was a letter dated February 27, 1902, written to Lee Yang from a niece named Mei Mei. I believe you've ..." she paused, "met her?"

I nodded.

"I thought so. She mentions you by name. It's in English by the way. Would you like to read it?"

"Oh, yes!" I said, too loud for the old house. Mrs. Snyder smiled.

"Handle it carefully, it's almost ninety years old," she said. "Think about that."

I took the letter and unfolded it. Isabel watched me as I read the careful printing that reminded me very much of Daniel's writing.

Dear Uncle,

I am so pleased that you have completed your studies and are now a doctor, the first Chinese doctor to gradu-ate from the University in San Francisco. Some day I know that women, even Chinese women, will be doctors in America. I would wish that time was coming soon, but I do not believe it so. Not soon enough for me.

I am thirteen years today. I know you remember my birth-day faithfully, but cannot come. I say it only for me. Thirteen years. I feel all grown up and still small.

I have now thought what I will do with my life. It is not

enough only to be married and be a mother. I want to do more. I will move to the wonderful town where you have become doctor and I will open a restaurant. Perhaps it will be the first Chinese restaurant in Berkeley. I have also chosen the name. It will be named after our visitor who gave me the idea that ghosts would eat Chinese food.

I often think about Mar-Jee and how her time is still so far off. We will never know about her and about what happened. Yet I think you are right. She was in balance and that is enough.

Please come back as early as you can. We have missed you.

Mei Mei

After finishing the letter, I started reading again at the top. When I finished, I set it down on the coffee table, thinking about what Mei Mei had said about me: "She was in balance and that is enough." I thought about that little bundle of energy who was so much in balance.

I saw Isabel tentatively reaching for the letter, but Mrs. Snyder quickly leaned forward and picked it up.

"It's so odd," she said, her voice soft, as if she were talking to herself. "I have a meeting here in ten minutes, coffee to make and thoughts to organize. We've almost finalized arrangements to move all of these books to their permanent home after twenty years here, but I can't help thinking about the diary and the letter. Somehow this strange circumstance that confronts us demands some kind of response, some change in our view of reality."

She carefully folded the letter and put it into the envelope.

"I can't figure out an appropriate response and I'm afraid my view of reality has grown stubbornly rigid over the years. What happened is impossible and yet the evidence that it happened is undeniable. I'm afraid that the impossibility will gradually overwhelm the undeniability and over time I will cease to believe."

She shook her head.

"In truth, I'm of two minds about this meeting. Certainly, it will be good if these invaluable materials are more accessible — and that was what I hoped for all along, but I've grown so possessive. It will be hard to say 'goodbye' to all of them." She hesitated. "And I worry about the wear and tear on this old paper." She shook her head. "But it's no longer my responsibility and I need to let go."

Mrs. Snyder slowly stood up and gestured toward the door.

"I should think that you would be eager to turn your minds to these reports you have to do. Yet, how will you use this very unscholarly material? That is a puzzle I'm glad to leave to younger and more pliable brains."

Mrs. Snyder opened the door. "Please, Margie, when your report is done, will you send me a copy? I would love to read it. Maybe I can even find a place for it in my shelves."

※ ※ ※

Then we were on the stairs outside and the door was closed. It felt like it had closed for good and I wondered how much more of the past Mrs. Snyder would be allowed to accumulate before her time would come. I had wanted to ask for that letter for myself. I felt like it was mine. After all, it mentioned me and it appeared because of me, but I knew Mrs. Snyder saw things differently. She knew the letter was history, not a possession of a single person. Maybe she wanted me to move on, that as important as the past few days were to me personally, they were history, too, and I needed to start thinking again about my future.

I didn't notice the steps down or the sidewalk. I'm

glad Isabel was with me because I would probably have walked right in front of cars as I crossed the street. I don't remember talking for a while, only that Isabel kept looking at me — not talking, but thinking very loudly about me.

We stopped at a phone booth and I called Isabel's mom. My father had called a little earlier, but just to check in. Thinking of my mom scared me all over again. What if the parasites had already done too much permanent damage? That was too awful to think about. I decided I would keep focused on her recovery and try not to think about the damage already done until I heard more.

I told Mrs. Molina we were done at Mrs. Snyder's but that we were hungry and we were going to stop for lunch on the way home.

"Who's hungry?" Isabel asked when I hung up.

"I am," I said. "Besides I'm anxious to meet some friends who have been expecting me for a long time."

Isabel tried to get me to tell her more, but I kept it to myself, letting her get annoyed with my secret. When we reached the restaurant, Isabel stopped at the door and looked in.

"Margie, why are we here?"

I looked at her and grinned. "For lunch, of course." I went through the door and Isabel followed me in.

"You know I usually understand you, but not this time."

I only smiled and let the door swing shut.

The lunchtime rush was over. People were busily cleaning off tables and resetting them with napkins carefully folded into flowers and planted in empty wineglasses. I looked around my favorite Chinese restaurant with an almost possessive curiosity. Isabel sat quietly watching me.

The hostess brought us to a table and we sat down. I had seldom been to a restaurant without an adult before. I began reading the menu, thinking about little Mei Mei and her wonderful egg rolls.

"Well, I know what I want, even though I'm not really hungry," Isabel said, looking around. "Where is everybody, anyway?"

I looked up. The restaurant was suddenly empty — no customers, no waitresses, nobody.

"Margie, this is weird. This isn't just slow service. This is the Twilight Zone again. Why does everything get so weird when you're around?"

"Well, Isabel, have you thought that maybe it's you and not me?" I asked.

"No!" she said quickly. "It's definitely you."

I laughed. "You're right."

"It doesn't seem to bother you that the restaurant would suddenly empty out after we sit down. What's going on? Do you know?"

"No," I said, "not exactly. But after reading that letter I just had to come here."

"What does this restaurant have to do with such an old letter?" Isabel asked.

"Mei Mei was planning to open a restaurant. She said it in the letter to Daniel. And it explains just about everything: the little girl who watched me, the fortune written in Chinese."

"Wait a …"

"I understand something now," I said, interrupting, "something that had been a real mystery. You know that my mom and dad came here on their first date and that they named me 'Marjorie' after the restaurant?"

"Yes. You've told me that several times."

"Well, you do realize what that means?" I asked. Just then the door to the kitchen squeaked open and I saw a small face looking out, a familiar face.

Isabel looked at the door as it closed again. When she turned back her expression was impatient.

"I'm not sure."

I nodded, waiting for her to work it through.

"I don't understand. What does all that have do with what happened on your birthday?"

"This *is* the restaurant Mei Mei started. Don't you see?" I said smiling.

Poor Isabel, I think she did see, but she was having a lot of trouble believing.

"She said in the letter she was going to name the restaurant after me." I pointed to the menu and spelled it, "M-a-r-J-e-e. She didn't know how to spell it."

"Really!"

"Yes! I'm named after the restaurant and … the restaurant's named after me."

"I don't believe it!"

I shook my head. "It's so confusing. Time isn't at all like I thought it was. It's like some kind of wheel." Maybe more like a river, I thought.

The door squeaked again, only this time it opened all the way. The little girl came out first, holding the hand of a woman a little younger than my mom. Following them came several other people. They came and gathered into a semi-circle by our table. Isabel was clearly uncomfortable and so were they.

The little girl finally stepped up to the table and looked closely at me.

"You are Mar-Jee, aren't you?"

I nodded and winked at Isabel.

She turned to the woman.

"See? I told you."

The woman smiled and looked down.

"We thought we would never meet you, but we have known that this was your time from the stories that have been told."

"It's very hard to understand, isn't it?" I said.

"Yes, very hard."

I found Isabel staring at me intently.

For one uncomfortable minute, no one said anything.

Then the little girl who had spied on me the night of my birthday spoke up.

"My name is Lee Mei. I am named after my great grandmother. You can call me Mei Mei if you like."

I smiled at her. She looked very much like the Mei Mei I had met 100 years ago.

"I have something to show you." Her voice was shy, reminding me even more of her ancestor. She reached out and took my hand. I held on as she pulled me to the back of the restaurant and through the swinging door. As we went through the door, I glanced back. Isabel was watching us with a look of awe.

We walked through the kitchen to a door that led into a small room in back. It was an office. The walls were covered with drawings. Among the many pictures I saw a few of people I recognized, one of Lin Sun, one of Daniel Lee, and one of Hana, Daniel Lee's older niece. I certainly recognized the drawing style. Of course, the original Mei Mei was the artist so there were no drawings of her.

"My great grandmother did these," Mei Mei told me.

"I know," I said. "I recognize her style. I watched her draw a picture of me."

Mei Mei gave me a look of pure adoration.

"But," I asked, "how did you know what I looked like?"

The office door was still open. Mei Mei reached out and swung it closed. On the back was my picture. I mean the one Mei Mei drew of me a hundred years ago. I remembered it distinctly, even the pain in my shoulder and leg when I couldn't stand to pose anymore. The picture that I had done of Mei Mei so long ago, yellowed and cracked, but still as amateurish as ever, was hanging on the door below. It had not improved with age.

Mei Mei pointed to it and we both laughed.

"That is the only picture of my great grandmother," Mei Mei said. "I can't tell. Do I look like her?"

I bent down and looked at her face — and smiled.

"You look just like her — and neither of you look anything like my drawing."

Mei Mei positively beamed.

⋙ ⋙ ⋙

As we walked back through the restaurant, I saw that almost everyone had returned to work, but they all smiled and nodded as Mei Mei led me back to the table. Mei Mei's mother was sitting with Isabel. She looked up.

"Remember I told you that Mei Mei had drawn a picture of me?"

Isabel nodded.

"They have it back there. That's why they recognized me when I came in."

Isabel nodded slowly.

"It was only Mei Mei who recognized you at first," Mei Mei's mother said. "She pointed you out to us. It was funny as we ran back and forth to look at the picture, comparing it to you. It was a very good picture, much like you."

"Why didn't you say something to me?"

Mei's mother shook her head. "We could tell that you hadn't made your great journey yet so it would not have done any good. In fact, we worried what would happen if we told you about it before you went. Would that have then changed things? We all talked about it, but we didn't know. We worried about the balance."

I nodded and even Isabel seemed to be getting some of it.

"You must understand …" Her voice turned suddenly quiet. I looked at her, but she looked away almost shyly. "We think of you as family, as an ancestor. It is a funny idea, but it does not seem a wrong idea. There are many stories about you that are told among the many branches of the family descended from Daniel, from Lin Sun and from Lee Mei. For one hundred years our family has looked forward to this day."

I blushed and looked down. Mei Mei was tugging on my sleeve.

"I must ask you a question."

"Yes, Mei Mei."

"Did my great grandmother always want to start a restaurant?"

I frowned, thinking about the question. Was I the reason that the original Mei Mei started a restaurant? It was hard to believe — and I didn't really know.

"You know," I began, "I only knew your ancestor for one day. I don't feel I can tell you much."

Mei Mei looked deeply disappointed. "What can you tell me?"

"I can tell you what she said in a letter she wrote to Daniel Lee."

"What? What did she say?" She was very excited.

"She hoped that a Chinese woman could become a doctor here in the United States someday and she was sorry the time would not come soon enough for her."

Mei Mei's eyes sparkled like stars.

"Then I will become a doctor," she said.

< 12 >

EVERYTHING IN BALANCE

It was Saturday, June 18, the day of my Bat Mitzvah. I sat in one of the big carved chairs on the bima, my arms resting on the burgundy leather arm rests, my fingers curled around the carved wood. I wondered how many Bar and Bat Mitzvahs had sat here in this chair, not quite fitting it, almost adults but still children.

I had completed my Torah portion, stumbling and soft at first, but my voice growing in strength as my mouth became comfortable again with Hebrew. I was thinking about the sermon I would be making soon, worrying about it, and not just from performance anxiety. Suddenly I was sure that what I had struggled with for weeks was trite and stupid. Could I get up there and actually read those words? I began to feel dizzy. This was going to be awful, why hadn't I done a better job?

As I sat there, feeling my chest growing tight and my fear building, I looked up at the east-facing stained-glass windows. They sparkled with the morning brightness, and light streamed through, tinting the floating particles of dust with red, green, and blue.

When we'd left for temple at 9:00 that morning, the

sky was covered with clouds and the air was cool and damp. Now, less than an hour later, the sun was out and so energetic it was taking time out to color the dust in the air over the congregation.

I looked up to Rabbi Cohen who was suddenly quiet. He was looking at me, smiling, gesturing for me to come up. It was my turn.

I looked at my speech, written word for word, timed to be exactly eight minutes allowing for occasional breathing, three pauses for dramatic effect, and one brief pause for laughter. Then I looked again at the sun streaming through the colored glass. I left the speech face down on the chair next to me and began walking toward the bima. I saw Isabel, and Mr. and Mrs. Molina, and Mrs. Snyder sitting in one of the pews. Right behind them were my mom and dad and, sitting next to my dad, was Jonah in a suit with his hair slicked down. He was so cute. He gave me a high sign as I stepped behind the bima.

I took a deep breath. Something would come to me. All I had to do was believe in myself.

∿∿ ∿∿ ∿∿

The timer was buzzing downstairs and the image of me standing on the bima looking out over the congregation began to fade. I glanced out the window. It was a gray evening. Clouds had come in during the past hour and now there were wisps of fog drifting along the street. I turned on the light over my desk and looked at Dr. Albers's letter.

As I thought about the questions I asked her, I wasn't sure whether I'd simply wanted the answers for the book like I'd told her, or if there was something else I was trying to answer for myself. It was hard now as I thought about how close we came to losing Mom and how much she suffered during those last days of her illness before we discovered the final pages of the diary.

I picked up the letter and started reading again:

One thing I learned very clearly from your mother is what a wonderful person you are, quite apart from the fact that you can perform miraculous feats — or at least the one miraculous feat your mother needed. I look forward to meeting you, perhaps when your mother comes for her next follow-up visit.

All of us offer our heartfelt apologies that you all had to suffer so much before we were able to effectively intervene. Of course, your mother was at our facility for only three days before we began the treatment that arrested the progress of the disease, but every day exacted such a terrible price. The final diagnosis matched what you told us. The Latin name for the condition is Cerebral Baylisascaris larva migrans. I want the best for all my patients, but it's easy to see why you are so devoted to your mother, apparently devoted enough to make a miracle for her. It brings tears to my eyes to think about it. Although, as doctors, we always do everything medically possible for our patients, all of us on the team were hoping and praying for her and pursuing every diagnostic lead we could think of. I want you to know that within an hour of the time your father called with your diagnosis, the whole team was assembled at your mother's side, scrubbed and ready to do the biopsy, even though many of us had just gotten home from our shifts.

I'm sure you appreciated Shelley's new hairstyle. We did the best we could to leave her some hair to work with. Of course, it will grow back with time. It's probably coming back by now. Your mother said she had fast-growing hair.

Once we pinned down the diagnosis, my biggest fear was your mother's recovery. There's still a lot we don't know about the extent of the nerve damage. Certainly nerve damage doesn't heal like other tissue damage, but I've never seen a patient more motivated. She made amazing progress between her release and her first return visit and I understand from your father that she's improving every day. She has one of the best physical therapists in the world there in Berkeley and, if anyone can find a way to forge new nerve pathways to replace the old ones, it's Shelley Gould.

Please feel free to call if you have questions and best of luck on your book. I'll want a signed copy.

Dr. Katherine Albers, MD

I set down the letter and looked out at the darkened street. I turned back to the words, my words on the computer screen. The story was there inside me, all of it, waiting for me to let it out. My eyes strayed back to the title. I moved the cursor, then backspaced over the letters and hesitated, thinking about Daniel Lee, what he looked like and the way he spoke. Suddenly I remembered what he'd said that first night on the trip to Stockton and I set my fingers on the keys, tapping in my slow, regular rhythm: "T-i-m-e L-i-k-e a R-i-v-e-r."

I sat back and looked at it, satisfied for now. Maybe that would be the final title and maybe not. Mom's humming drifted in from down the hall. I didn't know what the future held for her or for me, but her humming was the most comforting thing I had heard in weeks, maybe in years.

I moved the cursor to the end of the page. My eyes strayed again to the bulletin board where I'd tacked up my fortune with Daniel Lee's translation: 'Believe in yourself.' I settled my fingers on the home row and started typing ...

～～～ ～～～ ～～～

It was Saturday night and I was with Mom and Dad at Mar-Jee's Fine Mandarin Cuisine ...

Biographies

Randy Perrin has been writing professionally for twenty years as a reporter, technical writer and grant writer. Though raised as a Minnesotan, he has spent most of his adult years in the Bay Area. He currently lives just a half block down and around the corner from Margie's house in Berkeley (but don't look for it), taking seriously the ages-old novelist's advice to write about what you know, at least (in this case) geographically. He ignored the advice about not writing in your day job if you want to be a novelist. Words need to work together in much the same way in all writing, and he did his apprenticeship making technical documents and proposals that said just what they needed to say.

Randy began working on *Time Like a River* with his daughter Hannah after a May Day visit to Ardenwood Regional Park, a restored working farm, in 1993. Tova, his older daughter, joined the project a little later. Randy's desire to collaborate with his daughters came from his need to talk stories through with someone and his desire to involve the family in an exciting, long-term project. They proved to be wonderful at listening, suggesting, dictating sections of stories, editing and rewriting.

Hannah Perrin started her collaboration on the book when she was seven years old. She has loved the process and now, at eleven years old, takes proud responsibility for the result. The many times her father spoke carelessly about "my book" she was quick to correct him.

She brought drafts of the book to her third-grade teacher at Park Day School in Oakland. Her teacher consumer-tested the book by reading it to the class. Hannah recorded the kids comments and brought them home for consideration. Hannah has proven herself with a red pen, editing, commenting, and suggesting and she is wonderful at helping to unravel plot problems and correct character flaws.

Tova Perrin started on the collaboration several months later than Hannah but with real determination. She was nine years old at the start of the three-year writing project. Tova's grasp of the complexities of plotting and her creative zest were major influences in the final form of the book. She also helped to ensure Margie and Isabel spoke appropriately for their ages. Unfortunately, her father was not ready to make a wholesale endorsement of Teenspeak, so Margie may not be completely authentic, but she is understandable. Tova now attends Willard Middle School, Margie's school, where she is perfecting her Teenspeak while she continues to struggle with the dialect we call 'The King's English.'

Many people have wondered how much of the actual writing Hannah and Tova did, including what specific sections they wrote. In addition to their contributions in developing the story and characters and in shaping how the story was told, they also added words, phrases and passages that improved the overall story. After so many revisions, it's hard to find any part of the book that wasn't influenced by all of the authors.

Karen Tanner is Hannah's and Tova's mother and the unsung hero of the project. Supporting the project initially because it was such a wonderful experience for the kids, she reached the point when she began to recognize that her family was creating a real live book. Then she joined in with enthusiasm and a sharp editorial eye.

Readers who enjoy *Time Like a River* might want to watch for the next book we hope to publish, tentatively titled: *Remembering Mbina.*

Unfortunately, the raccoon parasites are not a creation of fiction. In her work at the Parent Infant Program of Children's Hospital, Oakland, Karen came to know a child who was diagnosed with cerebral Baylisascaris larva migrans, a progressive neurological condition resulting from a parasite normally found in raccoons. Symptoms are similar to those associated with the ingestion of certain toxic substances, encephalitis, Parkinson's Disease and other diseases of the nervous system.

〜〜 〜〜 〜〜

Hannah: I have been working on the book for about three years and have experienced many changes in the process. I enjoyed many parts of making the book but especially editing, reading and working sessions and collaborating with my family. I also enjoyed helping to fix plot or character problems and taking the book into my old third grade class at Park Day School and reading it.

Writing the book has developed an entire new world for me that many people don't get to experience. It is a world of fiction, imagination and, most of all, learning.

The hardest part for me was finding time when my whole family was able to work on the story.

Presently, I'm working on another book with my father and a book of my own which is about a girl who wants to be the first girl on her school's boy's baseball team. To make the team she not only needs to overcome gender discrimination, she needs to find her true self.

~~~ ~~~ ~~~

Tova: My dad once said, "You know, girls, this book will be published."

And you know what? That really motivated me! Now I know if I stick to anything long enough, I can succeed. For instance, the book took three years, but now we are all working on new books with new ideas. Working on the book has given me a lot of confidence and I feel now that I have made an impact.

Writing this book took a lot of planning, writing, editing, and rewriting. It was a lot of work, but it was also fun. I enjoyed presenting my ideas and hearing my dad's and sister's ideas, then trying to work out the options.

What I learned while writing this book will help me out in the future, particularly working on my new book which is about a girl from the farm who isn't fitting in with the popular, upper-class town girls. It's also about a prank that goes *very* wrong.